WE DON'T
KNOW WHAT'S
HAPPENED
OUT THERE
SINCE THEY PUT
US HERE.
OR HOW MANY
GENERATIONS
HAVE DIED
SINCE THEY DID.
WE COULD
BE THE LAST
PEOPLE
LEFT.

ALLEGIANT

"I'VE BEEN RECEIVING disturbing reports of a rebel organization among us." She looks up, raising an eyebrow. "People always organize into groups. That's a fact of our existence. I just didn't expect it to happen this quickly."

"What kind of organization?"

"The kind that wants to leave the city," she says. "They released some kind of manifesto this morning. They call themselves the Allegiant." When she sees my confused look, she adds, "Because they're *allied* with the original purpose of our city, see?"

"The original purpose—you mean, what was in the Edith Prior video? That we should send people outside when the city has a large Divergent population?"

"That, yes. But also living in factions. The Allegiant claim that we're meant to be in factions because we've been in them since the beginning." She shakes her head. "Some people will always fear change. But we can't indulge them."

"You'll be up all night with **DIVERGENT**, a brainy thrill-ride of a novel."

—BOOKPAGE

"The imaginative action and glimpses of a sprawling conspiracy are serious attention-grabbers, and the portrait of a shattered, derelict, overgrown, and abandoned Chicago is evocative as ever."

—HOLLYWOODCRUSH.MTV.COM

"Author Roth tells the riveting and complex story of a teenage girl forced to choose between her routinized, selfless family and the adventurous, unrestrained future she longs for. A memorable, unpredictable journey from which it is nearly impossible to turn away."

—PUBLISHERS WEEKLY (STARRED REVIEW)

"With brisk pacing and lavish flights of imagination, **DIVERGENT** clearly has thrills, but it also movingly explores a more common adolescent anxiety—the painful realization that coming into one's own sometimes means leaving family behind, both ideologically and physically."

—NEW YORK TIMES BOOK REVIEW

"Nonstop, adrenaline-heavy action. Packed with stunning twists and devastating betrayals."

—BCCB

"**DIVERGENT** is really an extended metaphor about the trials of modern adolescence: constantly having to take tests that sort and rank you among your peers, facing separation from your family, agonizing about where you fit in, and deciding when (or whether) to reveal the ways you may diverge from the group."

—WALL STREET JOURNAL

"This gritty, paranoid world is built with careful details and intriguing scope. The plot clips along at an addictive pace, with steady jolts of brutal violence and swoony romance. Fans snared by the ratcheting suspense will be unable to resist speculating on their own factional allegiance."

—KIRKUS REVIEWS

"Roth knows how to write. The novel's love story, intricate plot, and unforgettable setting work in concert to deliver a novel that will rivet fans of the first book."

—PUBLISHERS WEEKLY

"In this addictive sequel to the acclaimed **DIVERGENT**, a bleak postapocalyptic Chicago collapses into all-out civil war. Another spectacular cliff-hanger."

—*KIRKUS REVIEWS*

"**INSURGENT** explores several critical themes, including the importance of family and the crippling power of grief at its loss."

—*SLJ*

"Roth's plotting is intelligent and complex. Dangers, suspicion, and tension lurk around every corner, and the chemistry between Tris and Tobias remains heart-poundingly real. . . . This final installment will capture and hold attention until the divisive final battle has been waged."

—*PUBLISHERS WEEKLY*

"The tragic conclusion, although shocking, is thematically consistent; the bittersweet epilogue offers a poignant hope."

—*KIRKUS REVIEWS*

ANNIVERSARY EDITION

ALLEGIANT

VERONICA ROTH

KATHERINE TEGEN BOOKS
An Imprint of HarperCollins Publishers

Katherine Tegen Books is an imprint of HarperCollins Publishers.

Allegiant
www.epicreads.com

Library of Congress Control Number: 2013941315

ISBN 978-0-06-304053-3

Typography by Joel Tippie

23 24 25 26 27 LBC 7 6 5 4 3

❖

Revised paperback edition, 2021

To Jo,
who guides and steadies me

*Every question that can be answered must be
answered or at least engaged.
Illogical thought processes must be
challenged when they arise.
Wrong answers must be corrected.
Correct answers must be affirmed.*

—From the Erudite faction manifesto

CHAPTER ONE

I PACE IN our cell in Erudite headquarters, her words echoing in my mind: *My name will be Edith Prior, and there is much I am happy to forget.*

"So you've *never* seen her before? Not even in pictures?" Christina says, her wounded leg propped up on a pillow. She was shot during our desperate attempt to reveal the Edith Prior video to our city. At the time we had no idea what it would say, or that it would shatter the foundation we stand on, the factions, our identities. "Is she a grandmother or an aunt or something?"

"I told you, no," I say, turning when I reach the wall. "Prior is—was—my father's name, so it would have to be on his side of the family. But Edith is an Abnegation name, and my father's relatives must have been Erudite, so . . ."

"So she must be older," Cara says, leaning her head against the wall. From this angle she looks just like her brother, Will, my friend, the one I shot. Then she straightens, and the ghost of him is gone. "A few generations back. An ancestor."

"Ancestor." The word feels old inside me, like crumbling brick. I touch one wall of the cell as I turn around. The panel is cold and white.

My ancestor, and this is the inheritance she passed to me: freedom from the factions, and the knowledge that my Divergent identity is more important than I could have known. My existence is a signal that we need to leave this city and offer our help to whoever is outside it.

"I want to know," Cara says, running her hand over her face. "I need to know how long we've been here. Would you stop pacing for *one minute*?"

I stop in the middle of the cell and raise my eyebrows at her.

"Sorry," she mumbles.

"It's okay," Christina says. "We've been in here way too long."

It's been days since Evelyn mastered the chaos in the lobby of Erudite headquarters with a few short commands and had all the prisoners hustled away to cells on the third floor. A factionless woman came to doctor our wounds and distribute painkillers, and we've eaten and showered several times, but no one has told us what's going on outside. No matter how forcefully I've asked them.

"I thought Tobias would come by now," I say, dropping to the edge of my cot. "Where *is* he?"

"Maybe he's still angry that you lied to him and went behind his back to work with his father," Cara says.

I glare at her.

"Four wouldn't be that petty," Christina says, either to chastise Cara or to reassure me, I'm not sure. "Something's probably going on that's keeping him away. He told you to trust him."

In the chaos, when everyone was shouting and the factionless were trying to push us toward the staircase, I curled my fingers in the hem of his shirt so I wouldn't lose him. He took my wrists in his hands and pushed me away, and those were the words he said. *Trust me. Go where they tell you.*

"I'm trying," I say, and it's true. I'm trying to trust him. But every part of me, every fiber and every nerve, is straining toward freedom, not just from this cell but from the prison of the city beyond it.

I need to see what's outside the fence.

CHAPTER TWO

TOBIAS

I CAN'T WALK these hallways without remembering the days I spent as a prisoner here, barefoot, pain pulsing inside me every time I moved. And with that memory is another one, one of waiting for Beatrice Prior to go to her death, of my fists against the door, of her legs slung across Peter's arms when he told me she was just drugged.

I hate this place.

It isn't as clean as it was when it was the Erudite compound; now it is ravaged by war, bullet holes in the walls and the broken glass of shattered lightbulbs everywhere. I walk over dirty footprints and beneath flickering lights to her cell and I am admitted without question, because I bear the factionless symbol—an empty circle—on a black band around my arm and Evelyn's features on my face. Tobias Eaton was a shameful name, and now it is a powerful one.

Tris crouches on the ground inside, shoulder to shoulder with Christina and diagonal from Cara. My Tris should look pale and small—she *is* pale and small, after all—but instead the room is full of her.

Her round eyes find mine and she is on her feet, her arms wound tightly around my waist and her face against my chest.

I squeeze her shoulder with one hand and run my other hand over her hair, still surprised when her hair stops above her neck instead of below it. I was happy when she cut it, because it was hair for a warrior and not a girl, and I knew that was what she would need.

"How'd you get in?" she says in her low, clear voice.

"I'm Tobias Eaton," I say, and she laughs.

"Right. I keep forgetting." She pulls away just far enough to look at me. There is a wavering expression in her eyes, like she is a heap of leaves about to be scattered by the wind. "What's happening? What took you so long?"

She sounds desperate, pleading. For all the horrible memories this place carries for me, it carries more for her, the walk to her execution, her brother's betrayal, the fear serum. I have to get her out.

Cara looks up with interest. I feel uncomfortable, like I have shifted in my skin and it doesn't quite fit anymore. I hate having an audience.

"Evelyn has the city under lockdown," I say. "No one goes a step in any direction without her say-so. A few days ago she gave a speech about uniting against our oppressors, the people outside."

"Oppressors?" Christina says. She takes a vial from her pocket and dumps the contents into her mouth—painkillers for the bullet wound in her leg, I assume.

I slide my hands into my pockets. "Evelyn—and a lot of people, actually—think we shouldn't leave the city just to help a bunch of people who shoved us in here so they could use us later. They want to try to heal the city and solve our own problems instead of leaving to solve other people's. I'm paraphrasing, of course," I say. "I suspect that opinion is very convenient for my mother, because as long as we're all contained, she's in charge. The second we leave, she loses her hold."

"Great." Tris rolls her eyes. "Of course she would choose the most selfish route possible."

"She has a point." Christina wraps her fingers around the vial. "I'm not saying I don't want to leave the city and see what's out there, but we've got enough going on here. How are we supposed to help a bunch of people we've never met?"

Tris considers this, chewing on the inside of her cheek. "I don't know," she admits.

My watch reads three o'clock. I've been here too long—long enough to make Evelyn suspicious. I told her I came to break things off with Tris, that it wouldn't take much time. I'm not sure she believed me.

I say, "Listen, I mostly came to warn you—they're starting the trials for all the prisoners. They're going to put you all under truth serum, and if it works, you'll be convicted as traitors. I think we would all like to avoid that."

"Convicted as *traitors*?" Tris scowls. "How is revealing the truth to our entire city an act of betrayal?"

"It was an act of defiance against your leaders," I say. "Evelyn and her followers don't want to leave the city. They won't thank you for showing that video."

"They're just like Jeanine!" She makes a fitful gesture, like she wants to hit something but there's nothing available. "Ready to do anything to stifle the truth, and for what? To be kings of their tiny little world? It's ridiculous."

I don't want to say so, but part of me agrees with my mother. I don't owe the people outside this city anything, whether I am Divergent or not. I'm not sure I want to offer myself to them to solve humanity's problems, whatever that means.

But I do want to leave, in the desperate way that an

animal wants to escape a trap. Wild and rabid. Ready to gnaw through bone.

"Be that as it may," I say carefully, "if the truth serum works on you, you will be convicted."

"*If* it works?" says Cara, narrowing her eyes.

"Divergent," Tris says to her, pointing at her own head. "Remember?"

"That's fascinating." Cara tucks a stray hair back into the knot just above her neck. "But atypical. In my experience, most Divergent can't resist the truth serum. I wonder why you can."

"You and every other Erudite who ever stuck a needle in me," Tris snaps.

"Can we focus, please? I would like to avoid having to break you out of prison," I say. Suddenly desperate for comfort, I reach for Tris's hand, and she brings her fingers up to meet mine. We are not people who touch each other carelessly; every point of contact between us feels important, a rush of energy and relief.

"All right, all right," she says, gently now. "What did you have in mind?"

"I'll get Evelyn to let you testify first, of the three of you," I say. "All you have to do is come up with a lie that will exonerate both Christina and Cara, and then tell it under truth serum."

"What kind of lie would do that?"

"I thought I would leave that to you," I say. "Since you're the better liar."

I know as I'm saying the words that they hit a sore spot in both of us. She lied to me so many times. She promised me she wouldn't go to her death in the Erudite compound when Jeanine demanded the sacrifice of a Divergent, and then she did it anyway. She told me she would stay home during the Erudite attack, and then I found her in Erudite headquarters, working with my father. I understand why she did all those things, but that doesn't mean we aren't still broken.

"Yeah." She looks at her shoes. "Okay, I'll think of something."

I set my hand on her arm. "I'll talk to Evelyn about your trial. I'll try to make it soon."

"Thank you."

I feel the urge, familiar now, to wrench myself from my body and speak directly into her mind. It is the same urge, I realize, that makes me want to kiss her every time I see her, because even a sliver of distance between us is infuriating. Our fingers, loosely woven a moment ago, now clutch together, her palm tacky with moisture, mine rough in places where I have grabbed too many handles on too many moving trains. Now she looks pale and small, but her eyes make me think of wide-open skies that I have never actually seen, only dreamed of.

"If you're going to kiss, do me a favor and tell me so I can look away," says Christina.

"We are," Tris says. And we do.

I touch her cheek to slow the kiss down, holding her mouth on mine so I can feel every place where our lips touch and every place where they pull away. I savor the air we share in the second afterward and the slip of her nose across mine. I think of something to say, but it is too intimate, so I swallow it. A moment later I decide I don't care.

"I wish we were alone," I say as I back out of the cell.

She smiles. "I almost always wish that."

As I shut the door, I see Christina pretending to vomit, and Cara laughing, and Tris's hands hanging at her sides.

CHAPTER THREE

TRIS

"I THINK YOU'RE all idiots." My hands are curled in my lap like a sleeping child's. My body is heavy with truth serum. Sweat collects on my eyelids. "You should be thanking me, not questioning me."

"We should thank you for defying the instructions of your faction leaders? Thank you for trying to prevent one of your faction leaders from killing Jeanine Matthews? You behaved like a traitor." Evelyn Johnson spits the word like a snake. We are in the conference room in Erudite headquarters, where the trials have been taking place. I have now been a prisoner for at least a week.

I see Tobias, half-hidden in the shadows behind his mother. He has kept his eyes averted since I sat in the she says, indicating a woman with gray streaks in her dark curly hair. "And my sister, Rose. Mom, Rose, this is my friend Tris, and my initiation instructor, Four."

"Obviously," Stephanie says. "We saw their interrogations several weeks ago, Christina."

"I know that, I was just being *polite*—"

"Politeness is deception in—"

"Yeah, yeah, I know." Christina rolls her eyes.

Her mother and sister, I notice, look at each other with something like wariness or anger or both. Then her sister turns to me and says, "So you killed Christina's boyfriend."

Her words create a cold feeling inside me, like a streak of ice divides one side of my body from the other. I want to answer, to defend myself, but I can't find the words.

"Rose!" Christina says, scowling at her. At my side, Tobias straightens, his muscles tensing. Ready for a fight, as always.

"I just thought we would air everything out," Rose says. "It wastes less time."

"And you wonder why I left our faction," Christina says. "Being honest doesn't mean you say whatever you want, whenever you want. It means that what you choose to say is true."

"A lie of omission is still a lie."

"You want the truth? I'm uncomfortable and don't want to be here right now. I'll see you guys later." She takes my arm and walks Tobias and me away from her family, shaking her head the whole time. "Sorry about that. They're not really the forgiving type."

"It's fine," I say, though it's not.

I thought that when I received Christina's forgiveness, the hard part of Will's death would be over. But when you kill someone you love, the hard part is never over. It just gets easier to distract yourself from what you've done.

My watch reads twelve o'clock. A door across the room opens, and in walk two lean silhouettes. The first is Johanna Reyes, former spokesperson of Amity, identifiable by the scar that crosses her face and the hint of yellow peeking out from under her black jacket. The second is another woman, but I can't see her face, just that she is wearing blue.

I feel a spike of terror. She looks almost like . . . Jeanine. *No, I saw her die. Jeanine is dead.*

The woman comes closer. She is statuesque and blond, like Jeanine. A pair of glasses dangles from her front pocket, and her hair is in a braid. An Erudite from head to foot, but not Jeanine Matthews.

Cara.

Cara and Johanna are the leaders of the Allegiant?

"Hello," Cara says, and all conversation stops. She

smiles, but on her the expression looks compulsory, like she's just adhering to a social convention. "We aren't supposed to be here, so I'm going to keep this meeting short. Some of you—Zeke, Tori—have been helping us for the past few days."

I stare at Zeke. *Zeke* has been helping Cara? I guess I forgot that he was once a Dauntless spy. Which is probably when he proved his loyalty to Cara—he had some kind of friendship with her before she left Erudite headquarters not long ago.

He looks at me, wiggles his eyebrows, and grins.

Johanna continues, "Some of you are here because we want to ask for your help. All of you are here because you don't trust Evelyn Johnson to determine the fate of this city."

Cara touches her palms together in front of her. "We believe in following the guidance of the city's founders, which has been expressed in two ways: the formation of the factions, and the Divergent mission expressed by Edith Prior, to send people outside the fence to help whoever is out there once we have a large Divergent population. We believe that even if we have not reached that Divergent population size, the situation in our city has become dire enough to send people outside the fence anyway.

"In accordance with the intentions of our city's founders, we have two goals: to overthrow Evelyn and the factionless so that we can reestablish the factions, and to send some of our number outside the city to see what's out there. Johanna will be heading up the former effort, and I will be heading up the latter, which is what we will mostly be focusing on tonight." She presses a loose strand of hair back into her braid. "Not many of us will be able to go, because a crowd that large would draw too much attention. Evelyn won't let us leave without a fight, so I thought it would be best to recruit people who I know to be experienced with surviving danger."

I glance at Tobias. We certainly are experienced with danger.

"Christina, Tris, Tobias, Tori, Zeke, and Peter are my selections," Cara says. "You have all proven your skills to me in one way or another, and it's for that reason that I'd like to ask you to come with me outside the city. You are under no obligation to agree, of course."

"Peter?" I demand, without thinking. I can't imagine what Peter could have done to "prove his skills" to Cara.

"He kept the Erudite from killing you," Cara says mildly. "Who do you think provided him with the technology to fake your death?"

I raise my eyebrows. I had never thought about it before—too much happened after my failed execution for me to dwell on the details of my rescue. But of course, Cara was the only well-known defector from Erudite at that time, the only person Peter would have known to ask for help. Who else could have helped him? Who else would have known how?

I don't raise another objection. I don't want to leave this city with Peter, but I'm too desperate to leave to make a fuss about it.

"That's a lot of Dauntless," a girl at the side of the room says, looking skeptical. She has thick eyebrows that don't stop growing in the middle, and pale skin. When she turns her head, I see black ink right behind her ear. A Dauntless transfer to Erudite, no doubt.

"True," Cara says. "But what we need right now are people with the skills to get out of the city unscathed, and I think Dauntless training makes them highly qualified for that task."

"I'm sorry, but I don't think I can go," Zeke says. "I couldn't leave Shauna here. Not after her sister just . . . well, you know."

"I'll go," Uriah says, his hand popping up. "I'm Dauntless. I'm a good shot. And I provide much-needed eye candy."

I laugh. Cara does not seem to be amused, but she nods. "Thank you."

"Cara, you'll need to get out of the city fast," the Dauntless-turned-Erudite girl says. "Which means you should get someone to operate the trains."

"Good point," Cara says. "Does anyone here know how to drive a train?"

"Oh. I do," the girl says. "Was that not implied?"

The pieces of the plan come together. Johanna suggests we take Amity trucks from the end of the railroad tracks out of the city, and she volunteers to supply them to us. Robert offers to help her. Stephanie and Rose volunteer to monitor Evelyn's movements in the hours before the escape, and to report any unusual behavior to the Amity compound by two-way radio. The Dauntless who came with Tori offer to find weapons for us. The Erudite girl prods at any weaknesses she sees, and so does Cara, and soon they are all shored up, like we have just built a secure structure.

There is only one question left. Cara asks it:

"When should we go?"

And I volunteer an answer:

"Tomorrow night."

CHAPTER NINE

TOBIAS

THE NIGHT AIR slips into my lungs, and I feel like it is one of my last breaths. Tomorrow I will leave this place and seek another.

Uriah, Zeke, and Christina start toward Erudite headquarters, and I hold Tris's hand to keep her back.

"Wait," I say. "Let's go somewhere."

"Go somewhere? But . . ."

"Just for a little while." I tug her toward the corner of the building. At night I can almost see what the water looked like when it filled the empty canal, dark and patterned with moonlit ripples. "You're with me, remember? They're not going to arrest you."

A twitch at the corner of her mouth—almost a smile.

Around the corner, she leans against the wall and I stand in front of her, the river at my back. She's wearing something dark around her eyes to make their color stand out, bright and striking.

"I don't know what to do." She presses her hands to her face, curling her fingers into her hair. "About Caleb, I mean."

"You don't?"

She moves one hand aside to look at me.

"Tris." I set my hands on the wall on either side of her face and lean into them. "You don't want him to die. I know you don't."

"The thing is . . ." She closes her eyes. "I'm so . . . *angry*. I try not to think about him because when I do I just want to . . ."

"I know. God, I know." My entire life I've daydreamed about killing Marcus. Once I even decided how I would do it—with a knife, so I could feel the warmth leave him, so I could be close enough to watch the light leave his eyes. Making that decision frightened me as much as his violence ever did.

"My parents would want me to save him, though." Her eyes open and lift to the sky. "They would say it's selfish to let someone die just because they wronged you. Forgive, forgive, forgive."

"This isn't about what they want, Tris."

"Yes, it is!" She presses away from the wall. "It's always about what they want. Because he belongs to them more than he belongs to me. And I want to make them proud of me. It's all I want."

Her pale eyes are steady on mine, determined. I have never had parents who set good examples, parents whose expectations were worth living up to, but she did. I can see them within her, the courage and the beauty they pressed into her like a handprint.

I touch her cheek, sliding my fingers into her hair. "I'll get him out."

"What?"

"I'll get him out of his cell. Tomorrow, before we leave." I nod. "I'll do it."

"Really? Are you sure?"

"Of course I'm sure."

"I . . ." She frowns up at me. "Thank you. You're . . . amazing."

"Don't say that. You haven't found out about my ulterior motives yet." I grin. "You see, I didn't bring you here to talk to you about Caleb, actually."

"Oh?"

I set my hands on her hips and push her gently back against the wall. She looks up at me, her eyes clear and eager. I lean in close enough to taste her breaths, but pull back when she leans in, teasing.

She hooks her fingers in my belt loops and pulls me against her, so I have to catch myself on my forearms. She tries to kiss me but I tilt my head to dodge her, kissing just under her ear, then along her jaw to her throat. Her skin is soft and tastes like salt, like a night run.

"Do me a favor," she whispers into my ear, "and never have pure motives again."

She puts her hands on me, touching all the places I am marked, down my back and over my sides. Her fingertips slip under the waistband of my jeans and hold me against her. I breathe against the side of her neck, unable to move.

Finally we kiss, and it is a relief. She sighs, and I feel a wicked smile creep across my face.

I lift her up, letting the wall bear most of her weight, and her legs drape around my waist. She laughs into another kiss, and I feel strong, but so does she, her fingers stern around my arms. The night air slips into my lungs, and I feel like it is one of my first breaths.

CHAPTER
TEN

TOBIAS

THE BROKEN BUILDINGS in the Dauntless sector look like doorways to other worlds. Ahead of me I see the Pire piercing the sky.

The pulse in my fingertips marks the passing seconds. The air still feels rich in my lungs, though summer is drawing to a close. I used to run all the time and fight all the time because I cared about muscles. Now my feet have saved me too often, and I can't separate running and fighting from what they are: a way to escape danger, a way to stay alive.

When I reach the building, I pace before the entrance to catch my breath. Above me, panes of glass reflect light in every direction. Somewhere up there is the chair I sat in while I was running the attack simulation, and a smear of Tris's father's blood on the wall. Somewhere up there, Tris's voice pierced the simulation I was under, and I felt her hand on my chest, drawing me back to reality.

I open the door to the fear landscape room and flip open the small black box that was in my back pocket to see the syringes inside. This is the box I have always used, padded around the needles; it is a sign of something sick inside me, or something brave.

I position the needle over my throat and close my eyes as I press down on the plunger. The black box clatters to the ground, but by the time I open my eyes, it has disappeared.

I stand on the roof of the Hancock building, near the zip line where the Dauntless flirt with death. The clouds are black with rain, and the wind fills my mouth when I open it to breathe. To my right, the zip line snaps, the wire cord whipping back and shattering the windows below me.

My vision tightens around the roof edge, trapping it in the center of a pinhole. I can hear my own exhales despite the whistling wind. I force myself to walk to the edge. The rain pounds against my shoulders and head, dragging me toward the ground. I tip my weight forward just a little and fall, my jaw clamped around my screams, muffled and suffocated by my own fear.

After I land, I don't have a second to rest before the walls close in around me, the wood slamming into my spine, and then my head, and then my legs. Claustrophobia. I pull my arms in to my chest, close my eyes, and try not to panic.

I think of Eric in his fear landscape, willing his terror into submission with deep breathing and logic. And Tris, conjuring weapons out of thin air to attack her worst nightmares. But I am not Eric, and I am not Tris. What am I? What do *I* need, to overcome my fears?

I know the answer, of course I do: I need to deny them the power to control me. I need to know that I am stronger than they are.

I breathe in and slam my palms against the walls to my left and right. The box creaks, and then breaks, the boards crashing to the concrete floor. I stand above them in the dark.

Amar, my initiation instructor, taught us that our fear landscapes were always in flux, shifting with our moods and changing with the little whispers of our nightmares. Mine was always the same, until a few weeks ago. Until I proved to myself that I could overpower my father. Until I discovered someone I was terrified to lose.

I don't know what I will see next.

I wait for a long time without anything changing. The room is still dark, the floor still cold and hard, my heart still beating faster than normal. I look down to check my watch and discover that it's on the wrong hand—I usually wear mine on my left, not my right, and my watchband isn't gray, it's black.

Then I notice bristly hairs on my fingers that weren't there before. The calluses on my knuckles are gone. I look down, and I am wearing gray slacks and a gray shirt; I am thicker around the middle and thinner through the shoulders.

I lift my eyes to a mirror that now stands in front of me. The face staring back at mine is Marcus's.

He winks at me, and I feel the muscles around my eye contracting as he does, though I didn't tell them to. Without warning, his—my—*our* arms jerk toward the glass and reach into it, closing around the neck of my reflection. But then the mirror disappears, and my—his—*our* hands are around our own throat, dark patches creeping into the edge of our vision. We sink to the ground, and the grip is as tight as iron.

I can't think. I can't think of a way out of this one.

By instinct, I scream. The sound vibrates against my hands. I picture those hands as mine really are, large with slender fingers and calloused knuckles from hours at the punching bag. I imagine my reflection as water running over Marcus's skin, replacing every piece of him with a piece of me. I remake myself in my own image.

I am kneeling on the concrete, gasping for air.

My hands tremble, and I run my fingers over my neck, my shoulders, my arms. Just to make sure.

I told Tris, on the train to meet Evelyn a few weeks ago, that Marcus was still in my fear landscape, but that he had changed. I spent a long time thinking about it; it crowded my thoughts every night before I slept and clamored for attention every time I woke. I was still afraid of him, I knew, but in a different way—I was no longer a child, afraid of the threat my terrifying father posed to my safety. I was a man, afraid of the threat he posed to my character, to my future, to my identity.

But even that fear, I know, does not compare to the one that comes next. Even though I know it's coming, I want to open a vein and drain the serum from my body rather than see it again.

A pool of light appears on the concrete in front of me. A hand, the fingers bent into a claw, reaches into the light, followed by another hand, and then a head, with stringy blond hair. The woman coughs and drags herself into the circle of light, inch by inch. I try to move toward her, to help her, but I am frozen.

The woman turns her face toward the light, and I see that she is Tris. Blood spills over her lips and curls around her chin. Her bloodshot eyes find mine, and she wheezes, "Help."

She coughs red onto the floor, and I throw myself toward her, somehow knowing that if I don't get to her soon, the light will leave her eyes. Hands wrap around my arms and shoulders and chest, forming a cage of flesh and bone, but I keep straining toward her. I claw at the hands holding me, but I only end up scratching myself.

I shout her name, and she coughs again, this time more blood. She screams for help, and I scream for her, and I don't hear anything, I don't feel anything, but my heartbeat, but my own terror.

She drops to the ground, tensionless, and her eyes roll back into her head. It's too late.

The darkness lifts. The lights return. Graffiti covers the walls of the fear landscape room, and across from me are the mirror-windows to the observation room, and in the corners are the cameras that record each session, all where they're supposed to be. My neck and back are covered in sweat. I wipe my face with the hem of my shirt and walk to the opposite door, leaving my black box with its syringe and needle behind.

I don't need to relive my fears anymore. All I need to do now is try to overcome them.

I know from experience that confidence alone can get a person into a forbidden place. Like the cells on the third floor of Erudite headquarters.

Not here, though, apparently. A factionless man stops me with the end of his gun before I reach the door, and I am nervous, choking.

"Where you going?"

I put my hand on his gun and push it away from my arm. "Don't point that thing at me. I'm here on Evelyn's orders. I'm going to see a prisoner."

"I didn't hear about any after-hours visits today."

I drop my voice low, so he feels like he's hearing a secret. "That's because she didn't want it on the record."

"Chuck!" someone calls out from the stairs above us. It's Therese. She makes a waving motion as she walks down. "Let him through. He's fine."

I nod to Therese and keep moving. The debris in the hallway has been swept clean, but the broken lightbulbs haven't been replaced, so I walk through stretches of darkness, like patches of bruises, on my way to the right cell.

When I reach the north corridor, I don't go straight to the cell, but rather to the woman who stands at the end. She is middle-aged, with eyes that droop at the edges and a mouth held in a pucker. She looks like everything exhausts her, including me.

"Hi," I say. "My name is Tobias Eaton. I'm here to collect a prisoner, on orders from Evelyn Johnson."

Her expression doesn't change when she hears my name, so for a few seconds I'm sure I'll have to knock her unconscious to get what I want. She takes a piece of crumpled paper from her pocket and flattens it against her left palm. On it is a list of prisoners' names and their corresponding room numbers.

"Name?" she says.

"Caleb Prior. 308A."

"You're Evelyn's son, right?"

"Yeah. I mean . . . yes." She doesn't seem like the kind of person who likes the word "yeah."

She leads me to a blank metal door with 308A on it—I wonder what it was used for when our city didn't require so many cells. She types in the code, and the door springs open.

"I guess I'm supposed to pretend I don't see what you're about to do?" she says.

She must think I'm here to kill him. I decide to let her.

"Yes," I say.

"Do me a favor and put in a good word for me with Evelyn. I don't want so many night shifts. The name's Drea."

"You got it."

She gathers the paper into her fist and shoves it back into her pocket as she walks away. I keep my hand on the door handle until she reaches her post again and turns to the side so she isn't facing me. It seems like she's done this a few times before. I wonder how many people have disappeared from these cells at Evelyn's command.

I walk in. Caleb Prior sits at a metal desk, bent over a book, his hair piled on one side of his head.

"What do you want?" he says.

"I hate to break this to you—" I pause. I decided a few hours ago how I wanted to handle this—I want to teach Caleb a lesson. And it will involve a few lies. "You know, actually, I kind of don't hate it. Your execution's been moved up a few weeks. To tonight."

That gets his attention. He twists in his chair and stares at me, his eyes wild and wide, like prey faced with a predator.

"Is that a joke?"

"I'm really bad at telling jokes."

"No." He shakes his head. "No, I have a few weeks, it's not *tonight*, no—"

"If you shut up, I'll give you an hour to adjust to this new information. If you don't shut up, I'll knock you out and shoot you in the alley outside before you wake up. Make your choice now."

Seeing an Erudite process something is like watching the inside of a watch, the gears all turning, shifting, adjusting, working together to form a particular function, which in this case is to make sense of his imminent demise.

Caleb's eyes shift to the open door behind me, and he seizes the chair, turning and swinging it into my body. The legs hit me, hard, which slows me down just enough to let him slip by.

I follow him into the hallway, my arms burning from where the chair hit me. I am faster than he is—I slam into his back and he hits the floor face-first, without bracing himself. With my knee against his back, I pull his wrists together and squeeze them into a plastic loop. He groans, and when I pull him to his feet, his nose is bright with blood.

Drea's eyes touch mine for just a moment, then move away.

I drag him down the hallway, not the way I came, but another way, toward an emergency exit. We walk down a flight of narrow stairs where the echo of our footsteps layers over itself, dissonant and hollow. Once I'm at the bottom, I knock on the exit door.

Zeke opens it, a stupid grin on his face.

"No trouble with the guard?"

"No."

"I figured Drea would be easy to get by. She doesn't care about anything."

"It sounded like she had looked the other way before."

"That doesn't surprise me. Is this Prior?"

"In the flesh."

"Why's he bleeding?"

"Because he's an idiot."

Zeke offers me a black jacket with a factionless symbol stitched into the collar. "I didn't know that idiocy caused people to just start spontaneously bleeding from the nose."

I wrap the jacket around Caleb's shoulders and fasten one of the buttons over his chest. He avoids my eyes.

"I think it's a new phenomenon," I say. "The alley's clear?"

"Made sure of it." Zeke holds out his gun, handle first. "Careful, it's loaded. Now it would be great if you would hit me so I'm more convincing when I tell the factionless you stole it from me."

"You want me to hit you?"

"Oh, like you've never wanted to. Just do it, Four."

I do like to hit people—I like the explosion of power and energy, and the feeling that I am untouchable because I can hurt people. But I hate that part of myself, because it is the part of me that is the most broken.

Zeke braces himself and I curl my hand into a fist.

"Do it fast, you pansycake," he says.

I decide to aim for the jaw, which is too strong to break but will still show a good bruise. I swing, hitting him right where I mean to. Zeke groans, clutching his face with both hands. Pain shoots up my arm, and I shake my hand out.

"Great." Zeke spits at the side of the building. "Well, I guess that's it."

"Guess so."

"I probably won't be seeing you again, will I? I mean, I know the others might come back, but you . . ." He trails off, but picks up the thought again a moment later. "Just seems like you'll be happy to leave it behind, that's all."

"Yeah, you're probably right." I look at my shoes. "You sure you won't come?"

"Can't. Shauna can't wheel around where you guys are going, and it's not like I'm gonna leave her, you know?" He touches his jaw, lightly, testing the skin. "Make sure Uri doesn't drink too much, okay?"

"Yeah," I say.

"No, I mean it," he says, and his voice dips down the way it always does when he's being serious, for once. "Promise you'll look out for him?"

It's always been clear to me, since I met them, that Zeke

and Uriah were closer than most brothers. They lost their father when they were young, and I suspect Zeke began to walk the line between parent and sibling after that. I can't imagine what it feels like for Zeke to watch him leave the city now, especially as broken by grief as Uriah is by Marlene's death.

"I promise," I say.

I know I should leave, but I have to stay in this moment for a little while, feeling its significance. Zeke was one of the first friends I made in Dauntless, after I survived initiation. Then he worked in the control room with me, watching the cameras and writing stupid programs that spelled out words on the screen or played guessing games with numbers. He never asked me for my real name, or why a first-ranked initiate ended up in security and instruction instead of leadership. He demanded nothing from me.

"Let's just hug already," he says.

Keeping one hand firm on Caleb's arm, I wrap my free arm around Zeke, and he does the same.

When we break apart, I pull Caleb down the alley, and can't resist calling back, "I'll miss you."

"You too, sweetie!"

He grins, and his teeth are white in the twilight. They are the last thing I see of him before I have to turn and set out at a trot for the train.

"You're going somewhere," says Caleb, between breaths. "You and some others."

"Yeah."

"Is my sister going?"

The question awakes inside me an animal rage that won't be satisfied by sharp words or insults. It will only be satisfied by smacking his ear hard with the flat of my hand. He winces and hunches his shoulders, preparing for a second strike.

I wonder if that's what I looked like when my father did it to me.

"She is not your sister," I say. "You betrayed her. You tortured her. You took away the only family she had left. And because . . . what? Because you wanted to keep Jeanine's secrets, wanted to stay in the city, safe and sound? You are a coward."

"I am not a coward!" Caleb says. "I knew if—"

"Let's go back to the arrangement where you keep your mouth closed."

"Fine," he says. "Where are you taking me, anyway? You can kill me just as well here, can't you?"

I pause. A shape moves along the sidewalk behind us, slippery in my periphery. I twist and hold up my gun, but the shape disappears into the yawn of an alley.

and you take away their motivation, or their ability to assert themselves. Take away their selfishness and you take away their sense of self-preservation. If you think about it, I'm sure you know exactly what I mean."

I tick off each quality in my mind as he says it—fear, low intelligence, dishonesty, aggression, selfishness. He *is* talking about the factions. And he's right to say that every faction loses something when it gains a virtue: the Dauntless, brave but cruel; the Erudite, intelligent but vain; the Amity, peaceful but passive; the Candor, honest but inconsiderate; the Abnegation, selfless but stifling.

"Humanity has never been perfect, but the genetic alterations made it worse than it had ever been before. This manifested itself in what we call the Purity War. A civil war, waged by those with damaged genes, against the government and everyone with pure genes. The Purity War caused a level of destruction formerly unheard of on American soil, eliminating almost half of the country's population."

"The visual is up," says one of the people at a desk in the control room.

A map appears on the screen above David's head. It is an unfamiliar shape, so I'm not sure what it's supposed to represent, but it is covered with patches of pink, red, and dark-crimson lights.

"This is our country before the Purity War," David says. "And *this* is after—"

The lights start to recede, the patches shrinking like puddles of water drying in the sun. Then I realize that the red lights were people—people, disappearing, their lights going out. I stare at the screen, unable to wrap my mind around such a substantial loss.

David continues, "When the war was finally over, the people demanded a permanent solution to the genetic problem. And that is why the Bureau of Genetic Welfare was formed. Armed with all the scientific knowledge at our government's disposal, our predecessors designed experiments to restore humanity to its genetically pure state."

"They called for genetically damaged individuals to come forward so that the Bureau could alter their genes. The Bureau then placed them in secure environments to settle in for the long haul, equipped with basic versions of the serums to help them control their society. They would wait for the passage of time—for the generations to pass, for each one to produce more genetically healed humans. Or, as you currently know them . . . the Divergent."

Ever since Tori told me the word for what I am—Divergent—I have wanted to know what it means. And here is the simplest answer I have received: "Divergent" means that my genes are healed. Pure. Whole. I should feel relieved to know the real answer at last. But I just feel like something is off, itching in the back of my mind.

I thought that "Divergent" explained everything that I am and everything that I could be. Maybe I was wrong.

I am starting to feel short of breath as the revelations begin to work their way into my mind and heart, as David peels the layers of lies and secrets away. I touch my chest to feel my heartbeat, to try to steady myself.

"Your city is one of those experiments for genetic healing, and by far the most successful one, because of the behavioral modification portion. The factions, that is." David smiles at us, like it's something we should be proud of, but I am not proud. They created us, they shaped our world, they told us what to believe.

If they told us what to believe, and we didn't come to it on our own, is it still true? I press my hand harder against my chest. *Steady.*

"The factions were our predecessors' attempt to incorporate a 'nurture' element to the experiment—they discovered that mere genetic correction was not enough to change the way people behaved. A new social order, combined with the genetic modification, was determined to be the most complete solution to the behavioral problems that the genetic damage had created." David's smile fades as he looks around at all of us. I don't know what he expected—for us to smile back? He continues, "The factions were later introduced to most of our other experiments, three of which are currently active. We have gone to great lengths to protect you, observe you, and learn from you."

Cara runs her hands over her hair, as if checking for loose strands. Finding none, she says, "So when Edith Prior said we were supposed to determine the cause of Divergence and come out and help you, that was . . ."

"'Divergent' is the name we decided to give to those who have reached the desired level of genetic healing," says David. "We wanted to make sure that the leaders of your city valued them. We didn't expect the leader of Erudite to start hunting them down—or for the Abnegation to even tell her what they were—and contrary to what Edith Prior said, we never *really* intended for you to send a Divergent army out to us. We don't, after all, truly need your help. We just need your healed genes to remain intact and to be passed on to future generations."

"So what you're saying is that if we're not Divergent, we're *damaged*," Caleb says. His voice is shaking. I never thought I would see Caleb on the verge of tears because of something like this, but he is.

Steady, I tell myself again, and take another deep, slow breath.

"*Genetically* damaged, yes," says David. "However, we were surprised to discover that the behavioral modification component of our city's experiment was quite effective—up until recently, it actually helped quite a bit with the behavioral problems that made the genetic manipulation so problematic to begin with. So generally, you would not be able to tell whether a person's genes were damaged or healed from their behavior."

"I'm smart," Caleb says. "So you're saying that because my ancestors were *altered* to be smart, I, their descendant, can't be fully compassionate. I, and every other genetically damaged person, am limited by my damaged genes. And the Divergent are not."

"Well," says David, lifting a shoulder. "Think about it."

Caleb looks at me for the first time in days, and I stare back. Is that the explanation for Caleb's betrayal—his damaged genes? Like a disease that he can't heal, and can't control? It doesn't seem right.

"Genes aren't everything," Amar says. "People, even genetically damaged people, make choices. That's what matters."

I think of my father, a born Erudite, not Divergent; a man who could not help but be smart, choosing Abnegation, engaging in a lifelong struggle against his own nature, and ultimately fulfilling it. A man warring with himself, just as I war with myself.

That internal war doesn't seem like a product of genetic damage—it seems completely, purely *human*.

I look at Tobias. He is so washed out, so slouched, he looks like he might pass out. He's not alone in his reaction: Christina, Peter, Uriah, and Caleb all look stunned. Cara has the hem of her shirt pinched between her fingers, and she is moving her thumb over the fabric, frowning.

"This is a lot to process," says David.

That is an understatement.

Beside me, Christina snorts.

"And you've all been up all night," David finishes, like there was no interruption. "So I'll show you to a place where you can get some rest and food."

"Wait," I say. I think of the photograph in my pocket, and how Zoe knew my name when she gave it to me. I think of what David said, about observing us and learning from us. I think of the rows of screens, blank, right in front of me. "You said you've been observing us. How?"

Zoe purses her lips. David nods to one of the people at the desks behind him. All at once, all the screens turn on, each of them showing footage from different cameras. On the ones nearest to me, I see Dauntless headquarters. The Merciless Mart. Millennium Park. The Hancock building. The Hub.

"You've always known that the Dauntless observe the

city with security cameras," David says. "Well, we have access to those cameras too."

They've been watching us.

+ + +

I think about leaving.

We walk past the security checkpoint on our way to wherever David is taking us, and I think about walking through it again, picking up my gun, and running from this place where they've been watching me. Since I was small. My first steps, my first words, my first day of school, my first kiss.

Watching, when Peter attacked me. When my faction was put under a simulation and turned into an army. When my parents died.

What else have they seen?

The only thing that stops me from going is the photograph in my pocket. I can't leave these people before I find out how they knew my mother.

David takes us through the compound to a carpeted area with potted plants on either side. The wallpaper is old and yellowed, peeling from the corners of the walls. We follow him into a large room with high ceilings and wood floors and lights that glow orange-yellow. There are cots arranged in two straight rows, with trunks beside them for what we brought with us, and large windows with elegant curtains on the opposite end of the room. When I get closer to them, I see that they're worn and frayed at the edges.

David tells us that this part of the compound was a hotel, connected to the airport by a tunnel, and this room was once the ballroom. Again the words mean nothing to us, but he doesn't seem to notice.

"This is just a temporary dwelling, of course. Once you decide what to do, we will settle you somewhere else, whether it's in this compound or elsewhere. Zoe will ensure that you are well taken care of," he says. "I will be back tomorrow to see how you're all doing."

I look back at Tobias, who is pacing back and forth in front of the windows, gnawing on his fingernails. I never realized he had that habit. Maybe he was never distressed enough to do it before.

I could stay and try to comfort him, but I need answers about my mother, and I'm not going to wait any longer. I'm sure that Tobias, of all people, will understand. I follow David into the hallway. Just outside the room he leans against the wall and scratches the back of his neck.

"Hi," I say. "My name is Tris. I believe you knew my mother."

He jumps a little, but eventually smiles at me. I cross my arms. I feel the same way I did when Peter pulled my towel away during Dauntless initiation, to be cruel:

exposed, embarrassed, angry. Maybe it's not fair to direct all of that at David, but I can't help it. He's the leader of this compound—of the Bureau.

"Yes, of course," he says. "I recognize you."

From where? The creepy cameras that followed my every move? I pull my arms tighter across my chest.

"Right." I wait a beat, then say, "I need to know about my mother. Zoe gave me a picture of her, and you were standing right next to her in it, so I figured you could help."

"Ah," he says. "Can I see the picture?"

I take it out of my pocket and offer it to him. He smooths it down with his fingertips, and there is a strange smile on his face as he looks at it, like he's caressing it with his eyes. I shift my weight from one foot to the other—I feel like I'm intruding on a private moment.

"She took a trip back to us once," he says. "Before she settled into motherhood. That's when we took this."

"*Back* to you?" I say. "Was she one of you?"

"Yes," David says simply, like it's not a word that changes my entire world. "She came from this place. We sent her into the city when she was young to resolve a problem in the experiment."

"So she knew," I say, and my voice shakes, but I don't know why. "She *knew* about this place, and what was outside the fence."

David looks puzzled, his bushy eyebrows furrowed. "Well, of course."

The shaking moves down my arms and into my hands, and soon my entire body is shuddering, as if rejecting some kind of poison that I've swallowed, and the poison is knowledge, the knowledge of this place and its screens and all the lies I built my life on. "She knew you were *watching* us at every moment . . . watching as she *died* and my father died and everyone started killing each other! And did you send in someone to help her, to help me? No! No, all you did was take notes."

"Tris . . ."

He tries to reach for me, and I push his hand away. "Don't call me that. You shouldn't know that name. You shouldn't know anything about us."

Shivering, I walk back into the room.

+ + +

Back inside, the others have picked their beds and put their things down. It's just us in here, no intruders. I lean against the wall by the door and push my palms down the front of my pants to get the sweat off.

No one seems to be adjusting well. Peter lies facing the wall. Uriah and Christina sit side by side, having a conversation in low voices. Caleb is massaging his temples with his fingertips. Tobias is still pacing and gnawing on his fingernails. And Cara is on her own, dragging her hand over her face. For the first time since I met her, she looks upset, the Erudite armor gone.

I sit down across from her. "You don't look so good."

Her hair, usually smooth and perfect in its knot, is disheveled. She glowers at me. "That's kind of you to say."

"Sorry," I say. "I didn't mean it that way."

"I know." She sighs. "I'm . . . I'm an Erudite, you know."

I smile a little. "Yeah, I know."

"No." Cara shakes her head. "It's the only thing I am. Erudite. And now they've told me that's the result of some kind of flaw in my genetics . . . and that the factions themselves are just a mental prison to keep us under control. Just like Evelyn Johnson and the factionless said." She pauses. "So why form the Allegiant? Why bother to come out here?"

I didn't realize how much Cara had already cleaved to the idea of being an Allegiant, loyal to the faction system, loyal to our founders. For me it was just a temporary identity, powerful because it could get me out of the city. For her the attachment must have been much deeper.

"It's still good that we came out here," I say. "We found out the truth. That's not valuable to you?"

"Of course it is," Cara says softly. "But it means I need

other words for what I am."

Just after my mother died, I grabbed hold of my Divergence like it was a hand outstretched to save me. I needed that word to tell me who I was when everything else was coming apart around me. But now I'm wondering if I need it anymore, if we ever really *need* these words, "Dauntless," "Erudite," "Divergent," "Allegiant," or if we can just be friends or lovers or siblings, defined instead by the choices we make and the love and loyalty that binds us.

"Better check on him," Cara says, nodding to Tobias.

"Yeah," I say.

I cross the room and stand in front of the windows, staring at what we can see of the compound, which is just more of the same glass and steel, pavement and grass and fences. When he sees me, he stops pacing and stands next to me instead.

"You all right?" I say to him.

"Yeah." He sits on the windowsill, facing me, so we're at eye level. "I mean, no, not really. Right now I'm just thinking about how meaningless it all was. The faction system, I mean."

He rubs the back of his neck, and I wonder if he's thinking about the tattoos on his back.

"We put everything we had into it," he says. "All of us. Even if we didn't realize we were doing it."

"That's what you're thinking about?" I raise my eyebrows. "Tobias, they were *watching* us. Everything that happened, everything we did. They didn't intervene, they just invaded our privacy. Constantly."

He rubs his temple with his fingertips. "I guess. That's not what's bothering me, though."

I must give him an incredulous look without meaning to, because he shakes his head. "Tris, I worked in the Dauntless control room. There were cameras everywhere, all the time. I tried to warn you that people were watching you during your initiation, remember?"

I remember his eyes shifting to the ceiling, to the corner. His cryptic warnings, hissed between his teeth. I never realized he was warning me about cameras—it just never occurred to me before.

"It used to bother me," he says. "But I got over it a long time ago. We always thought we were on our own, and now it turns out we were right—they left us on our own. That's just the way it is."

"I guess I don't accept that," I say. "If you see someone in trouble, you should help them. Experiment or not. And . . . God." I cringe. "All the things they saw."

He smiles at me, a little.

"What?" I demand.

"I was just thinking of some of the things they saw,"

he says, putting his hand on my waist. I glare at him for a moment, but I can't sustain it, not with him grinning at me like that. Not knowing that he's trying to make me feel better. I smile a little.

I sit next to him on the windowsill, my hands wedged between my legs and the wood. "You know, the Bureau setting up the factions is not much different than what we thought happened: A long time ago, a group of people decided that the faction system would be the best way to live—or the way to get people to live the best lives they could."

He doesn't respond at first, just chews on the inside of his lip and looks at our feet, side by side on the floor. My toes brush the ground, not quite reaching it.

"That helps, actually," he says. "But there's so much that was a lie, it's hard to figure out what was true, what was real, what matters."

I take his hand, slipping my fingers between his. He touches his forehead to mine.

I catch myself thinking, *Thank God for this*, out of habit, and then I understand what he's so concerned about. What if my parents' God, their whole belief system, is just something concocted by a bunch of scientists to keep us under control? And not just their beliefs about God and whatever else is out there, but about right and wrong, about selflessness? Do all those things have to change because we know how our world was made?

I don't know.

The thought rattles me. So I kiss him—slowly, so I can feel the warmth of his mouth and the gentle pressure and his breaths as we pull away.

"Why is it," I say, "that we always find ourselves surrounded by people?"

"I don't know," he says. "Maybe because we're stupid."

I laugh, and it's laughter, not light, that casts out the darkness building within me, that reminds me I am still alive, even in this strange place where everything I've ever known is coming apart. I know some things—I know that I'm not alone, that I have friends, that I'm in love. I know where I came from. I know that I don't want to die, and for me, that's something—more than I could have said a few weeks ago.

+ + +

That night we push our cots just a little closer together, and look into each other's eyes in the moments before we fall asleep. When he finally drifts off, our fingers are twisted together in the space between the beds.

I smile a little, and let myself go too.

CHAPTER SIXTEEN

TOBIAS

THE SUN STILL hasn't completely set when we fall asleep, but I wake a few hours later, at midnight, my mind too busy for rest, swarming with thoughts and questions and doubts. Tris released me earlier, and her fingers now brush the floor. She is sprawled over the mattress, her hair covering her eyes.

I shove my feet into my shoes and walk the hallways, shoelaces slapping the carpets. I am so accustomed to the Dauntless compound that I am not used to the creak of wooden floors beneath me—I am used to the scrape and echo of stone, and the roar and pulse of water in the chasm.

A week into my initiation, Amar—worried that I was becoming increasingly isolated and obsessive—invited me to join some of the older Dauntless for a game of Dare.

For my dare, we went back to the Pit for me to get my first tattoo, the patch of Dauntless flames covering my rib cage. It was agonizing. I relished every second of it.

I reach the end of one hallway and find myself in an atrium, surrounded by the smell of wet earth. Everywhere plants and trees are suspended in water, the same way they were in the Amity greenhouses. In the center of the room is a tree in a giant water tank, lifted high above the floor so I can see the tangle of roots beneath it, strangely human, like nerves.

"You're not nearly as vigilant as you used to be," Amar says from behind me. "Followed you all the way here from the hotel lobby."

"What do you want?" I tap the tank with my knuckles, sending ripples through the water.

"I thought you might like an explanation for why I'm not dead," he says.

"I thought about it," I say. "They never let us see your body. It wouldn't be that hard to fake a death if you never show the body."

"Sounds like you've got it all figured out." Amar claps his hands together. "Well, I'll just go, then, if you're not curious. . . ."

I cross my arms.

Amar runs a hand over his black hair, tying it back with a rubber band. "They faked my death because I was

Divergent, and Jeanine had started killing the Divergent. They tried to save as many as they could before she got to them, but it was tricky, you know, because she was always a step ahead."

"Are there others?" I say.

"A few," he says.

"Any named Prior?"

Amar shakes his head. "No, Natalie Prior is actually dead, unfortunately. She was the one who helped me get out. She also helped this other guy too . . . George Wu. Know him? He's on a patrol right now, or he would have come with me to get you. His sister is still inside the city."

The name clutches at my stomach.

"Oh God," I say, and I lean into the tank wall.

"What? You know him?"

I shake my head.

I can't imagine it. There were just a few hours between Tori's death and our arrival. On a normal day, a few hours can contain long stretches of watch-checking, of empty time. But yesterday, just a few hours placed an impenetrable barrier between Tori and her brother.

"Tori is his sister," I say. "She tried to leave the city with us."

"*Tried* to," repeats Amar. "Ah. Wow. That's . . ."

Both of us are quiet for a while. George will never get to reunite with his sister, and she died thinking he had been murdered by Jeanine. There isn't anything to say—at least, not anything that's worth saying.

Now that my eyes have adjusted to the light, I can see that the plants in this room were selected for beauty, not practicality—flowers and ivy and clusters of purple or red leaves. The only flowers I've ever seen are wildflowers, or apple blossoms in the Amity orchards. These are more extravagant than those, vibrant and complex, petals folded into petals. Whatever this place is, it has not needed to be as pragmatic as our city.

"That woman who found your body," I say. "Was she just . . . lying about it?"

"People can't really be trusted to lie consistently." He quirks his eyebrows. "Never thought I would say that phrase—it's true, anyway. She was reset—her memory was altered to include me jumping off the Pire, and the body that was planted wasn't actually me. But it was too messed up for anyone to notice."

"She was reset. You mean, with the Abnegation serum."

"We call it 'memory serum,' since it doesn't technically just belong to the Abnegation, but yeah. That's the one."

I was angry with him before. I'm not really sure why. Maybe I was just angry that the world had become such a complicated place, that I have never known even a fraction of the truth about it. Or that I allowed myself to grieve for someone who was never really gone, the same way

I grieved for my mother all the years I thought she was dead. Tricking someone into grief is one of the cruelest tricks a person can play, and it's been played on me twice.

But as I look at him, my anger ebbs away, like the changing of the tide. And standing in the place of my anger is my initiation instructor and friend, alive again.

I grin.

"So you're alive," I say.

"More importantly," he says, pointing at me, "you are no longer upset about it."

He grabs my arm and pulls me into an embrace, slapping my back with one hand. I try to return his enthusiasm, but it doesn't come naturally—when we break apart, my face is hot. And judging by how he bursts into laughter, it's also bright red.

"Once a Stiff, always a Stiff," he says.

"Whatever," I say. "So do you like it here, then?"

Amar shrugs. "I don't really have a choice, but yeah, I like it fine. I work in security, obviously, since that's all I was trained to do. We'd love to have you, but you're probably too good for it."

"I haven't quite resigned myself to staying here just yet," I say. "But thanks, I guess."

"There's nowhere better out there," he says. "All the other cities—that's where most of the country lives, in these big metropolitan areas, like our city—are dirty and dangerous, unless you know the right people. Here at least there's clean water and food and safety."

I shift my weight, uncomfortable. I don't want to think about staying here, making this my home. I already feel trapped by my own disappointment. This is not what I imagined when I thought of escaping my parents and the bad memories they gave me. But I don't want to disturb the peace with Amar now that I finally feel like I have my friend back, so I just say, "I'll take that under advisement."

"Listen, there's something else you should know."

"What? More resurrections?"

"It's not exactly a resurrection if I was never dead, is it?" Amar shakes his head. "No, it's about the city. Someone heard it in the control room today—Marcus's trial is scheduled for tomorrow morning."

I knew it was coming—I knew Evelyn would save him for last, would savor every moment she spent watching him squirm under truth serum like he was her last meal. I just didn't realize that I would be able to see it, if I wanted to. I thought I was finally free of them, all of them, forever.

"Oh," is all I can say.

I still feel numb and confused when I walk back to the dormitory later and crawl back into bed. I don't know what I'll do.

CHAPTER SEVENTEEN

TRIS

I WAKE JUST before the sun. No one else stirs in their cot—
Tobias's arm is draped over his eyes, but his shoes are now
on, like he got up and walked around in the middle of the
night. Christina's head is buried beneath her pillow. I lay
for a few minutes, finding patterns in the ceiling, then
put on my shoes and run my fingers through my hair to
flatten it.

The hallways in the compound are empty except for a
few stragglers. I assume they are just finishing the night
shift, because they are hunched over screens, their chins
propped on their hands, or slumped against broomsticks,
barely remembering to sweep. I put my hands in my
pockets and follow the signs to the entrance. I want to get

encased in plastic and paper and have white labels. The room is full of the sound of crinkling and ripping.

"How do you guys like it here so far?" she asks us.

"It's been an adjustment," I say.

"Yeah, I know what you mean." Nita smiles at me. "I came from one of the other experiments—the one in Indianapolis, the one that failed. Oh, you don't know where Indianapolis is, do you? It's not far from here. Less than an hour by plane." She pauses. "That won't mean anything to you either. You know what? It's not important."

She takes a syringe and needle from its plastic-paper wrapping, and Tris tenses.

"What's that for?" Tris says.

"It's what will enable us to read your genes," Matthew says. "Are you okay?"

"Yeah," Tris says, but she's still tense. "I just . . . don't like to be injected with strange substances."

Matthew nods. "I swear it's just going to read your genes. That's all it does. Nita can vouch for it."

Nita nods.

"Okay," Tris says. "But . . . can I do it to myself?"

"Sure," Nita says. She prepares the syringe, filling it with whatever they intend to inject us with, and offers it to Tris.

"I'll give you the simplified explanation of how this

works," Matthew says as Nita brushes Tris's arm with antiseptic. The smell is sour, and it nips at the inside of my nose.

"The fluid is packed with microcomputers. They are designed to detect specific genetic markers and transmit the data to a computer. It will take them about an hour to give me as much information as I need, though it would take them much longer to read all your genetic material, obviously."

Tris sticks the needle into her arm and presses the plunger.

Nita beckons my arm forward and drags the orange-stained gauze over my skin. The fluid in the syringe is silver-gray, like fish scales, and as it flows into me through the needle, I imagine the microscopic technology chewing through my body, reading me and analyzing me. Beside me, Tris holds a cotton ball to her pricked skin and offers me a small smile.

"What are the . . . microcomputers?" Matthew nods, and I continue. "What are they looking for, exactly?"

"Well, when our predecessors at the Bureau inserted 'corrected' genes into your ancestors, they also included a genetic tracker, which is basically something that shows us that a person has achieved genetic healing. In this case, the genetic tracker is awareness during simulations—it's something we can easily test for, which shows us if your genes are healed or not. That's one of the reasons why everyone in the city has to take the aptitude test at sixteen—if they're aware during the test, that shows us that they might have healed genes."

I add the aptitude test to a mental list of things that were once so important to me, cast aside because it was just a ruse to get these people the information or result they wanted.

I can't believe that awareness during simulations, something that made me feel powerful and unique, something Jeanine and the Erudite *killed* people for, is actually just a sign of genetic healing to these people. Like a special code word, telling them I'm in their genetically healed society.

Matthew continues, "The only problem with the genetic tracker is that being aware during simulations and resisting serums doesn't necessarily mean that a person is Divergent, it's just a strong correlation. Sometimes people will be aware during simulations or be able to resist serums even if they still have damaged genes." He shrugs. "That's why I'm interested in your genes, Tobias. I'm curious to see if you're actually Divergent, or if your simulation awareness just makes it look like you are."

Nita, who is clearing the counter, presses her lips together like she is holding words inside her mouth. I feel suddenly uneasy. There's a chance I'm not actually Divergent?

"All that's left is to sit and wait," Matthew says. "I'm going to go get breakfast. Do either of you want something to eat?"

Tris and I both shake our heads.

"I'll be back soon. Nita, keep them company, would you?"

Matthew leaves without waiting for Nita's response, and Tris sits on the examination table, the paper crinkling beneath her and tearing where her leg hangs over the edge. Nita puts her hands in her jumpsuit pockets and looks at us. Her eyes are dark, with the same sheen as a puddle of oil beneath a leaking engine. She hands me a cotton ball, and I press it to the bubble of blood inside my elbow.

"So you came from a city experiment," says Tris. "How long have you been here?"

"Since the Indianapolis experiment was disbanded, which was about eight years ago. I could have integrated into the greater population, outside the experiments, but that felt too overwhelming." Nita leans against the counter. "So I volunteered to come here. I used to be a janitor. I'm moving through the ranks, I guess."

She says it with a certain amount of bitterness. I suspect that here, as in Dauntless, there is a limit to her climb through the ranks, and she is reaching it earlier than she would like to. The same way I did, when I chose my job in the control room.

"And your city, it didn't have factions?" Tris says.

"No, it was the control group—it helped them to figure out that the factions were actually effective by comparison. It had a lot of rules, though—curfew, wake-up times, safety regulations. No weapons allowed. Stuff like that."

"What happened?" I say, and a moment later I wish I hadn't asked, because the corners of Nita's mouth turn down, like the memory hangs heavy from each side.

"Well, a few of the people inside still knew how to make weapons. They made a bomb—you know, an explosive— and set it off in the government building," she says. "Lots of people died. And after that, the Bureau decided our experiment was a failure. They erased the memories of the bombers and relocated the rest of us. I'm one of the only ones who wanted to come here."

"I'm sorry," Tris says softly. Sometimes I still forget to look for the gentler parts of her. For so long all I saw was the strength, standing out like the wiry muscles in her arms or the black ink marking her collarbone with flight.

"It's all right. It's not like you guys don't know about stuff like this," says Nita. "With what Jeanine Matthews did, and all."

"Why haven't they shut our city down?" Tris says. "The

same way they did to yours?"

"They might still shut it down," says Nita. "But I think the Chicago experiment, in particular, has been a success for so long that they'll be a little reluctant to just ditch it now. It was the first one with factions."

I take the cotton ball away from my arm. There is a tiny red dot where the needle went in, but it isn't bleeding anymore.

"I like to think I would have chosen Dauntless," says Nita. "But I don't think I would have had the stomach for it."

"You'd be surprised what you have the stomach for, when you have to," Tris says.

I feel a pang in the middle of my chest. She's right. Desperation can make a person do surprising things. We would both know.

+ + +

Matthew returns right at the hour mark, and he sits at the computer for a long time after that, his eyes flicking back and forth as he reads the screen. A few times he makes a revelatory noise, a "hmm!" or an "ah!" The longer he waits to tell us something, anything, the more tense my muscles become, until my shoulders feel like they are made of stone instead of flesh. Finally he looks up and turns the screen around so we can see what's on it.

"This program helps us to interpret the data in an understandable way. What you see here is a simplified depiction of a particular DNA sequence in Tris's genetic material," he says.

The picture on the screen is a complicated mass of lines and numbers, with certain parts selected in yellow and red. I can't make any sense of the picture beyond that—it is above my level of comprehension.

"These selections here suggest healed genes. We wouldn't see them if the genes were damaged." He taps certain parts of the screen. I don't understand what he's pointing at, but he doesn't seem to notice, caught up in his own explanation. "These selections over here indicate that the program also found the genetic tracker, the simulation awareness. The combination of healed genes and simulation awareness genes is just what I expected to see from a Divergent. Now, this is the strange part."

He touches the screen again, and the screen changes, but it remains just as confusing, a web of lines, tangled threads of numbers.

"This is the map of Tobias's genes," Matthew says. "As you can see, he has the right genetic components for simulation awareness, but he doesn't have the same 'healed' genes that Tris does."

My throat is dry, and I feel like I've been given bad news, but I still haven't entirely grasped what that bad news is.

"What does that mean?" I ask.

"It means," Matthew says, "that you are not Divergent. Your genes are still damaged, but you have a genetic anomaly that allows you to be aware during simulations anyway. You have, in other words, the appearance of a Divergent without actually being one."

I process the information slowly, piece by piece. I'm not Divergent. I'm not like Tris. I'm genetically damaged.

The word "damaged" sinks inside me like it's made of lead. I guess I always knew there was something wrong with me, but I thought it was because of my father, or my mother, and the pain they bequeathed to me like a family heirloom, handed down from generation to generation. And this means that the one good thing my father had— his Divergence—didn't reach me.

I don't look at Tris—I can't bear it. Instead I look at Nita. Her expression is hard, almost angry.

"Matthew," she says. "Don't you want to take this data to your lab to analyze?"

"Well, I was planning on discussing it with our subjects here," Matthew says.

"I don't think that's a good idea," Tris says, sharp as a blade.

Matthew says something I don't really hear; I'm listening to the thump of my heart. He taps the screen again, and the picture of my DNA disappears, so the screen is blank, just glass. He leaves, instructing us to visit his lab if we want more information, and Tris, Nita, and I stand in the room in silence.

"It's not that big a deal," Tris says firmly. "Okay?"

"You don't get to tell me it's not a big deal!" I say, louder than I mean to be.

Nita busies herself at the counter, making sure the containers there are lined up, though they haven't moved since we first came in.

"Yeah, I do!" Tris exclaims. "You're the same person you were five minutes ago and four months ago and eighteen years ago! This doesn't change anything about you."

I hear something in her words that's right, but it's hard to believe her right now.

"So you're telling me this affects nothing," I say. "The truth affects nothing."

"What truth?" she says. "These people tell you there's something wrong with your genes, and you just believe it?"

"It was right there." I gesture to the screen. "You saw it."

"I also see you," she says fiercely, her hand closing around my arm. "And I know who you are."

I shake my head. I still can't look at her, can't look at anything in particular. "I . . . need to take a walk. I'll see you later."

"Tobias, wait—"

I walk out, and some of the pressure inside me releases as soon as I'm not in that room anymore. I walk down the cramped hallway that presses against me like an exhale, and into the sunlit halls beyond it. The sky is bright blue now. I hear footsteps behind me, but they're too heavy to belong to Tris.

"Hey." Nita twists her foot, making it squeak against the tile. "No pressure, but I'd like to talk to you about all this . . . genetic-damage stuff. If you're interested, meet me here tonight at nine. And . . . no offense to your girl or anything, but you might not want to bring her."

"Why?" I say.

"She's a GP—genetically pure. So she can't understand that—well, it's hard to explain. Just trust me, okay? She's better off staying away for a little while."

"Okay."

"Okay." Nita nods. "Gotta go."

I watch her run back toward the gene therapy room, and then I keep walking. I don't know where I'm going, exactly, just that when I walk, the frenzy of information I've learned in the past day stops moving quite so fast, stops shouting quite so loud inside my head.

CHAPTER
NINETEEN

TRIS

I DON'T GO after him, because I don't know what to say.

When I found out I was Divergent, I thought of it as a secret power that no one else possessed, something that made me different, better, stronger. Now, after comparing my DNA to Tobias's on a computer screen, I realize that "Divergent" doesn't mean as much as I thought it did. It's just a word for a particular sequence in my DNA, like a word for all people with brown eyes or blond hair.

I lean my head into my hands. But these people still think it means something—they still think it means I'm healed in a way that Tobias is not. And they want me to just trust that, believe it.

Well, I don't. And I'm not sure why Tobias does—why

he's so eager to believe that he is damaged.

I don't want to think about it anymore. I leave the gene therapy room just as Nita is walking back to it.

"What did you say to him?" I say.

She's pretty. Tall but not too tall, thin but not too thin, her skin rich with color.

"I just made sure he knew where he was going," she says. "It's a confusing place."

"It certainly is." I start toward—well, I don't know where I'm going, but it's away from Nita, the pretty girl who talks to my boyfriend when I'm not there. Then again, it's not like it was a long conversation.

I spot Zoe at the end of the hallway, and she waves me toward her. She looks more relaxed now than she did earlier this morning, her forehead smooth instead of creased, her hair loose over her shoulders. She shoves her hands into the pockets of her jumpsuit.

"I just told the others," she says. "We've scheduled a plane ride in two hours for those who want to go. Are you up for it?"

Fear and excitement squirm together in my stomach, just like they did before I was strapped in on the zip line atop the Hancock building. I imagine hurtling into the air in a car with wings, the energy of the engine and the rush of wind through all the spaces in the walls and the possibility, however slight, that something will fail and I will plummet to my death.

"Yes," I say.

"We're meeting at gate B14. Follow the signs!" She flashes a smile as she leaves.

I look through the windows above me. The sky is clear and pale, the same color as my own eyes. There is a kind of inevitability in it, like it has always been waiting for me, maybe because I relish height while others fear it, or maybe because once you have seen the things that I have seen, there is only one frontier left to explore, and it is above.

+ + +

The metal stairs leading down to the pavement screech with each of my footsteps. I have to tilt my head back to look at the airplane, which is bigger than I expected it to be, and silver-white. Just below the wing is a huge cylinder with spinning blades inside it. I imagine the blades sucking me in and spitting me out the other side, and shudder a little.

"How can something that big stay in the sky?" Uriah says from behind me.

I shake my head. I don't know, and I don't want to think about it. I follow Zoe up another set of stairs, this one connected to a hole in the side of the plane. My hand shakes when I grab the railing, and I look over my shoulder one last time, to check if Tobias caught up to us. He isn't there. I haven't seen him since the genetic test.

I duck when I go through the hole, though it's taller than my head. Inside the airplane are rows and rows of seats covered in ripped, fraying blue fabric. I choose one near the front, next to a window. A metal bar pushes against my spine. It feels like a chair skeleton with barely any flesh to support it.

Cara sits behind me, and Peter and Caleb move toward the back of the plane and sit near each other, next to the window. I didn't know they were friends. It seems fitting, given how despicable they both are.

"How old is this thing?" I ask Zoe, who stands near the front.

"Pretty old," she says. "But we've completely redone the important stuff. It's a nice size for what we need."

"What do you use it for?"

"Surveillance missions, mostly. We like to keep an eye on what's happening in the fringe, in case it threatens what's happening in here." Zoe pauses. "The fringe is a large, sort of chaotic place between Chicago and the nearest government-regulated metropolitan area, Milwaukee, which is about a three-hour drive from here."

I would like to ask what exactly *is* happening in the

fringe, but Uriah and Christina sit in the seats next to me, and the moment is lost. Uriah puts an armrest down between us and leans over me to look out the window.

"If the Dauntless knew about this, everyone would be getting in line to learn how to drive it," he says. "Including me."

"No, they would be strapping themselves to the wings." Christina pokes his arm. "Don't you know your own faction?"

Uriah pokes her cheek in response, then turns back to the window again.

"Have either of you seen Tobias lately?" I say.

"No, haven't seen him," Christina says. "Everything okay?"

Before I can answer, an older woman with lines around her mouth stands in the aisle between the rows of seats and claps her hands.

"My name is Karen, and I'll be flying this plane today!" she announces. "It may seem frightening, but remember: The odds of us crashing are actually much lower than the odds of a car crash."

"So are the odds of survival if we *do* crash," Uriah mutters, but he's grinning. His dark eyes are alert, and he looks giddy, like a child. I haven't seen him this way since Marlene died. He's handsome again.

Karen disappears into the front of the plane, and Zoe

sits across the aisle from Christina, twisting around to call out instructions like "Buckle your seat belts!" and "Don't stand up until we've reached our cruising altitude!" I'm not sure what cruising altitude is, and she doesn't explain it, in true Zoe fashion. It was almost a miracle that she remembered to explain the fringe earlier.

The plane starts to move backward, and I'm surprised by how smooth it feels, like we're already floating over the ground. Then it turns and glides over the pavement, which is painted with dozens of lines and symbols. My heart beats faster the farther we go away from the compound, and then Karen's voice speaks through an intercom: "Prepare for takeoff."

I clench the armrests as the plane lurches into motion. The momentum presses me back against the skeleton chair, and the view out the window turns into a smear of color. Then I feel it—the lift, the rising of the plane, and I see the ground stretching wide beneath us, everything getting smaller by the second. My mouth hangs open and I forget to breathe.

I see the compound, shaped like the picture of a neuron I once saw in my science textbook, and the fence that surrounds it. Around it is a web of concrete roads with buildings sandwiched between them.

And then suddenly, I can't even see the roads or the buildings anymore, because there is just a sheet of gray and green and brown beneath us, and farther than I can see in any direction is land, land, land.

I don't know what I expected. To see the place where the world ends, like a giant cliff hanging in the sky?

What I didn't expect is to know that I have been a person standing in a house that I can't even see from here. That I have walked a street among hundreds—thousands—of other streets.

What I didn't expect is to feel so, so small.

"We can't fly too high or too close to the city because we don't want to draw attention, so we'll observe from a great distance. Coming up on the left side of the plane is some of the destruction caused by the Purity War, before the rebels resorted to biological warfare instead of explosives," Zoe says.

I have to blink tears from my eyes before I can see it, what looks at first to be a group of dark buildings. Upon further examination, I realize that the buildings aren't supposed to be dark—they're charred beyond recognition. Some of them are flattened. The pavement between them is broken in pieces like a cracked eggshell.

It resembles certain parts of the city, but at the same time, it doesn't. The city's destruction could have been caused by people. This had to have been caused by something else, something bigger.

"And now you'll get a brief look at Chicago!" Zoe says.

"You'll see that some of the lake was drained so that we could build the fence, but we left as much of it intact as possible."

At her words I see the two-pronged Hub as small as a toy in the distance, the jagged line of our city interrupting the sea of concrete. And beyond it, a brown expanse—the marsh—and just past that . . . blue.

Once I slid down a zip line from the Hancock building and imagined what the marsh looked like full of water, blue-gray and gleaming under the sun. And now that I can see farther than I have ever seen, I know that far beyond our city's limits, it is just like what I imagined, the lake in the distance glinting with streaks of light, marked with the texture of waves.

The plane is silent around me except for the steady roar of the engine.

"Whoa," says Uriah.

"Shh," Christina replies.

"How big is it compared to the rest of the world?" Peter says from across the plane. He sounds like he's choking on each word. "Our city, I mean. In terms of land area. What percentage?"

"Chicago takes up about two hundred twenty-seven square miles," says Zoe. "The land area of the planet is a little less than two hundred million square miles. The percentage is . . . so small as to be negligible."

She delivers the facts calmly, as if they mean nothing to her. But they hit me square in the stomach, and I feel squeezed, like something is crushing me into myself. So much space. I wonder what it's like in the places beyond ours; I wonder how people live there.

I look out the window again, taking slow, deep breaths into a body too tense to move. And as I stare out at the land, I think that this, if nothing else, is compelling evidence for my parents' God, that our world is so massive that it is completely out of our control, that we cannot possibly be as large as we feel.

So small as to be negligible.

It's strange, but there's something in that thought that makes me feel almost . . . free.

+ + +

That evening, when everyone else is at dinner, I sit on the window ledge in the dormitory and turn on the screen David gave me. My hands tremble as I open the file labeled "Journal."

The first entry reads:

David keeps asking me to write down what I experienced. I think he expects it to be horrifying, maybe even wants it to be. I guess parts of it were, but they were bad for everyone, so it's not like I'm special.

I grew up in a single-family home in Milwaukee, Wisconsin. I never knew much about who was inside the territory outside the city (which everyone around here calls "the fringe"), just that I wasn't supposed to go there. My mom was in law enforcement; she was explosive and impossible to please. My dad was a teacher; he was pliable and supportive and useless. One day they got into it in the living room and things got out of hand, and he grabbed her and she shot him. That night she was burying his body in the backyard while I assembled a good portion of my possessions and left through the front door. I never saw her again.

Where I grew up, tragedy is all over the place. Most of my friends' parents drank themselves stupid or yelled too much or had stopped loving each other a long time ago, and that was just the way of things, no big deal. So when I left I'm sure I was just another item on a long list of awful things that had happened in our neighborhood in the past year.

I knew that if I went anyplace official, like to another city, the government types would just make me go home to my mom, and I didn't think I would ever be able to look at her without seeing the streak of blood my dad's head left on the living room carpet, so I didn't go anyplace official. I went to the fringe, where a whole bunch of people are living in a little colony made of tarp and aluminum in some of the postwar wreckage, living on scraps and burning old papers for warmth because the government can't provide, since they're spending all their resources trying to put us back together again, and have been for over a century after the war ripped us apart. Or they won't provide. I don't know.

One day I saw a grown man beating up one of the kids in the fringe, and I hit him over the head with a plank to get him to stop and he died, right there in the street. I was only thirteen. I ran. I got snatched by some guy in a van, some guy who looked like police. But he didn't take me to the side of the road to shoot me and he didn't take me to jail; he just took me to this secure area and tested my genes and told me all about the city experiments and how my genes were cleaner than other people's. He even showed me a map of my genes on a screen to prove it.

But I killed a man just like my mother did. David says it's okay because I didn't mean to, and because he was about to kill that little kid. But I'm pretty sure my mom didn't mean to kill my dad, either, so what difference does that make, meaning or not meaning to do something? Accident or on purpose, the result is the same, and that's one fewer life than there should be in the world.

That's what I experienced, I guess. And to hear David talk about it, it's like it all happened because a long, long time ago people tried to mess with human nature and ended up making it worse.

I guess that makes sense. Or I'd like it to.

My teeth dig into my lower lip. Here in the Bureau compound, people are sitting in the cafeteria right now, eating and drinking and laughing. In the city, they're probably doing the same thing. Ordinary life surrounds me, and I am alone with these revelations.

I clutch the screen to my chest. My mother was from here. This place is both my ancient and my recent history. I can feel her in the walls, in the air. I can feel her settled inside me, never to leave again. Death could not erase her; she is permanent.

The cold from the glass seeps through my shirt, and I shiver. Uriah and Christina walk through the door to the dormitory, laughing about something. Uriah's clear eyes and steady footsteps fill me with a sense of relief, and my eyes well up with tears all of a sudden. He and Christina both look alarmed, and they lean against the windows on either side of me.

"You okay?" she says.

I nod and blink the tears away. "Where have you guys been today?"

"After the plane ride we went and watched the screens in the control room for a while," Uriah says. "It's really weird to see what they're up to now that we're gone. Just more of the same—Evelyn's a jerk, so are all her lackeys, and so on—but it was like getting a news report."

"I don't think I'd like to look at those," I say. "Too . . . creepy and invasive."

Uriah shrugs. "I don't know, if they want to watch me scratch my butt or eat dinner, I feel like that says more about them than about me."

I laugh. "How often *are* you scratching your butt, exactly?"

He jostles me with his elbow.

"Not to derail the conversation from *butts*, which we can all agree is incredibly important—" Christina smiles a little. "But I'm with you, Tris. Just watching those screens made me feel awful, like I was doing something sneaky. I think I'll be staying away from now on."

She points to the screen in my lap, where the light still glows around my mother's words. "What's that?"

"As it turns out," I say, "my mother was from here. Well, she was from the world outside, but then she came here, and when she was fifteen, she was placed in Chicago as a Dauntless."

Christina says, "Your mother was from here?"

I nod. "Yeah. Insane. Even weirder, she wrote this journal and left it with them. That's what I was reading before you came in."

"Wow," Christina says softly. "That's good, right? I mean, that you get to learn more about her."

be given to people who don't want it."

"There's something to that," Matthew says. "But maybe it's time to grow out of that suspicion."

He reaches under the desk and takes out a book. It is thick, with a worn cover and frayed edges. On it is printed HUMAN BIOLOGY.

"It's a little rudimentary, but this book helped to teach me what it is to be human," he says. "To be such a complicated, mysterious piece of biological machinery, and more amazing still, to have the capacity to analyze that machinery! That is a special thing, unprecedented in all of evolutionary history. Our ability to know about ourselves and the world is what makes us human."

He hands me the book and turns back to the computer. I look down at the worn cover and run my fingers along the edge of the pages. He makes the acquisition of knowledge feel like a secret, beautiful thing, and an ancient thing. I feel like, if I read this book, I can reach backward through all the generations of humanity to the very first one, whenever it was—that I can participate in something many times larger and older than myself.

"Thank you," I say, and it's not for the book. It's for giving something back to me, something I lost before I was able to really have it.

+ + +

The lobby of the hotel smells like candied lemon and bleach, an acrid combination that burns my nostrils when I breathe it in. I walk past a potted plant with a garish flower blossoming among its branches, and toward the dormitory that has become our temporary home here. As I walk I wipe the screen with the hem of my shirt, trying to get rid of some of my fingerprints.

Caleb is alone in the dormitory, his hair tousled and his eyes red from sleep. He blinks at me when I walk in and toss the biology book onto my bed. I feel a sickening ache in my stomach and press the screen with our mother's file against my side. *He's her son. He has a right to read her journal, just like you.*

"If you have something to say," he says, "just say it."

"Mom lived here." I blurt it out like a long-held secret, too loud and too fast. "She came from the fringe, and they brought her here, and she lived here for a couple years, then went into the city to stop the Erudite from killing the Divergent."

Caleb blinks at me. Before I lose my nerve, I hold out the screen for him to take. "Her file is here. It's not very long, but you should read it."

He gets up and closes his hand around the glass. He's so much taller than he used to be, so much taller than I am. For a few years when we were children, I was the taller one, even though I was almost a year younger. Those were some of our best years, the ones where I didn't feel like he was bigger or better or smarter or more selfless than I was.

"How long have you known this?" he says, narrowing his eyes.

"It doesn't matter." I step back. "I'm telling you now. You can keep that, by the way. I'm done with it."

He wipes the screen with his sleeve and navigates with deft fingers to our mother's first journal entry. I expect him to sit down and read it, thus ending the conversation, but instead he sighs.

"I have something to show you, too," he says. "About Edith Prior. Come on."

It's her name, not my lingering attachment to him, that draws me after him when he starts to walk away.

He leads me out of the dormitory and down the hallway and around corners to a room far away from any that I have seen in the Bureau compound. It is long and narrow, the walls covered with shelves that bear identical blue-gray books, thick and heavy as dictionaries. Between the first two rows is a long wooden table with chairs tucked beneath it. Caleb flips the light switch, and pale light fills the room, reminding me of Erudite headquarters.

"I've been spending a lot of time here," he says. "It's the

record room. They keep some of the Chicago experiment data in here."

He walks along the shelves on the right side of the room, running his fingers over the book spines. He pulls out one of the volumes and lays it flat on the table, so it spills open, its pages covered in text and pictures.

"Why don't they keep all this on computers?"

"I assume they kept these records before they developed a sophisticated security system on their network," he says without looking up. "Data never fully disappears, but paper can be destroyed forever, so you can actually get rid of it if you don't want the wrong people to get their hands on it. It's safer, sometimes, to have everything printed out."

His green eyes shift back and forth as he searches for the right place, his fingers nimble, built for turning pages. I think of how he disguised that part of himself, wedging books between his headboard and the wall in our Abnegation house, until he dropped his blood in the Erudite water on the day of our Choosing Ceremony. I should have known, then, that he was a liar, with loyalty only to himself.

I feel that sickening ache again. I can hardly stand to be in here with him, the door closing us in, nothing but the table between us.

"Ah, here." He touches his finger to a page, then spins

the book around to show me.

It looks like a copy of a contract, but it's handwritten in ink:

I, Amanda Marie Ritter, of Peoria, Illinois, give my consent to the following procedures:

- The "genetic healing" procedure, as defined by the Bureau of Genetic Welfare: "a genetic engineering procedure designed to correct the genes specified as 'damaged' on page three of this form."

- The "reset procedure," as defined by the Bureau of Genetic Welfare: "a memory-erasing procedure designed to make an experiment participant more fit for the experiment."

I declare that I have been thoroughly instructed as to the risks and benefits of these procedures by a member of the Bureau of Genetic Welfare. I understand that this means I will be given a new background and a new identity by the Bureau and inserted into the experiment in Chicago, Illinois, where I will live out the remainder of my days.

I agree to reproduce at least twice to give my corrected genes the best possible chance of survival. I understand that I will be encouraged to do this when I am reeducated after the reset procedure.

I also give my consent for my children and my children's children, etc., to continue in this experiment until such time as the Bureau of Genetic Welfare deems it to be complete. They will be instructed in the false history that I myself will be given after the reset procedure.

Signed,

Amanda Marie Ritter

Amanda Marie Ritter. She was the woman in the video, Edith Prior, my ancestor.

I look up at Caleb, whose eyes are alight with knowledge, like there's a live wire running through each of them.

Our ancestor.

I pull out one of the chairs and sit. "She was Dad's ancestor?"

He nods and sits down across from me. "Seven generations back, yes. An aunt. Her brother is the one who carried on the Prior name."

"And this is . . ."

"It's a consent form," he says. "Her consent form for joining the experiment. The endnotes say that this was just a first draft—she was one of the original experiment designers. A member of the Bureau. There were only a few Bureau members in the original experiment; most of the people in the experiment weren't working for the government."

I read the words again, trying to make sense of them. When I saw her in the video, it seemed so logical that she would become a resident of our city, that she would immerse herself in our factions, that she would volunteer to leave behind everything she left behind. But that was before I knew what life was like outside the city, and it doesn't seem as horrific as what Edith described in her message to us.

She delivered a skillful manipulation in that video, which was intended to keep us contained and dedicated to the vision of the Bureau—*the world outside the city is badly broken, and the Divergent need to come out here and heal it.* It's not quite a lie, because the people in the Bureau do believe that healed genes will fix certain things, that if we integrate into the general population and pass our genes on, the world will be a better place. But they didn't need the Divergent to march out of our city like an army to fight injustice and save everyone, as Edith suggested. I wonder if Edith Prior believed her own words, or if she just said them because she had to.

There's a photograph of her on the next page, her mouth in a firm line, wisps of brown hair hanging around her face. She must have seen something terrible, to volunteer for her memory to be erased and her entire life remade.

"Do you know why she joined?" I say.

Caleb shakes his head. "The records suggest—though they're fairly vague on this front—that people joined the experiment so their families could escape extreme poverty—the families of the subjects were offered a monthly stipend for the subject's participation, for upward of ten years. But obviously that wasn't Edith's motivation, since she worked for the Bureau. I suspect something traumatic must have happened to her, something she was determined to forget."

I frown at her photograph. I can't imagine what kind of poverty would motivate a person to forget themselves and everyone they loved so their families could get a monthly stipend. I may have lived on Abnegation bread and vegetables for most of my life, with nothing to spare, but I was never that desperate. Their situation must have been much worse than anything I saw in the city.

I can't imagine why Edith was that desperate either. Or maybe it's just that she didn't have anyone to keep her memory for.

"I was interested in the legal precedent for giving consent on behalf of one's descendants," Caleb says. "I think it's an extrapolation of giving consent for one's children under eighteen, but it seems a little odd."

"I guess we all decide our children's fates just by making our own life decisions," I say vaguely. "Would we have chosen the same factions we did if Mom and Dad hadn't chosen Abnegation?" I shrug. "I don't know. Maybe we wouldn't have felt as stifled. Maybe we would have become different people."

The thought creeps into my mind like a slithering creature—*Maybe we would have become better people. People who don't betray their own sisters.*

I stare at the table in front of me. For the past few minutes it was easy to pretend that Caleb and I were just brother and sister again. But a person can only keep reality—and anger—at bay for so long before the truth comes back again. As I raise my eyes to his, I think of looking at him in just this way, when I was still a prisoner in Erudite headquarters. I think of being too tired to fight with him anymore, or to hear his excuses; too tired to care that my brother had abandoned me.

I ask tersely, "Edith joined Erudite, didn't she? Even though she took an Abnegation name?"

"Yes!" He doesn't seem to notice my tone. "In fact, most of our ancestors were in Erudite. There were a few Abnegation outliers, and one or two Candor, but the through line is fairly consistent."

I feel cold, like I might shiver and then shatter.

"So I suppose you've used this as an excuse in your twisted mind for what you did," I say steadily. "For joining

Erudite, for being loyal to them. I mean, if you were supposed to be one of them all along, then 'faction before blood' is an acceptable thing to believe, right?"

"Tris . . ." he says, and his eyes plead with me for understanding, but I do not understand. I won't.

I stand up. "So now I know about Edith and you know about our mother. Good. Let's just leave it at that, then."

Sometimes when I look at him I feel the ache of sympathy toward him, and sometimes I feel like I want to wrap my hands around his throat. But right now I just want to escape, and pretend this never happened. I walk out of the records room, and my shoes squeak on the tile floor as I run back to the hotel. I run until I smell sweet citrus, and then I stop.

Tobias is standing in the hallway outside the dormitory. I am breathless, and I can feel my heartbeat even in my fingertips; I am overwhelmed, teeming with loss and wonder and anger and longing.

"Tris," Tobias says, his brow furrowed with concern. "Are you all right?"

I shake my head, still struggling for air, and crush him against the wall with my body, my lips finding his. For a moment he tries to push me away, but then he must decide that he doesn't care if I'm all right, doesn't care if he's all right, doesn't care. We haven't been alone together in days. Weeks. Months.

His fingers slide into my hair, and I hold on to his arms to stay steady as we press together like two blades at a stalemate. He is stronger than anyone I know, and warmer than anyone else realizes; he is a secret that I have kept, and will keep, for the rest of my life.

He leans down and kisses my throat, hard, and his hands smooth over me, securing themselves at my waist. I hook my fingers in his belt loops, my eyes closing. In that moment I know exactly what I want; I want to peel away all the layers of clothing between us, strip away everything that separates us, the past and the present and the future.

I hear footsteps and laughter at the end of the hallway, and we break apart. Someone—probably Uriah—whistles, but I barely hear it over the pulsing in my ears.

Tobias's eyes meet mine, and it's like the first time I really looked at him during my initiation, after my fear simulation; we stare too long, too intently. "Shut up," I call out to Uriah, without looking away.

Uriah and Christina walk into the dormitory, and Tobias and I follow them, like nothing happened.

CHAPTER
TWENTY-THREE

TOBIAS

THAT NIGHT WHEN my head hits the pillow, heavy with thoughts, I hear something crinkle beneath my cheek. A note under my pillowcase.

T—

Meet me outside the hotel entrance at eleven. I need to talk to you.

—Nita

I look at Tris's cot. She's sprawled on her back, and there is a piece of hair covering her nose and mouth that shifts with each exhale. I don't want to wake her, but I feel strange, going to meet a girl in the middle of the night without telling her about it. Especially now that we're trying so hard to be honest with each other.

I check my watch. It's ten to eleven.

Nita's just a friend. You can tell Tris tomorrow. It might be urgent.

I push the blankets back and shove my feet into my shoes—I sleep in my clothes these days. I pass Peter's cot, then Uriah's. The top of a flask peeks out from beneath Uriah's pillow. I pinch it between my fingers and carry it toward the door, where I slide it under the pillow on one of the empty cots. I haven't been looking after him as well as I promised Zeke I would.

Once I'm in the hallway, I tie my shoes and smooth my hair down. I stopped cutting it like the Abnegation when I wanted the Dauntless to see me as a potential leader, but I miss the ritual of the old way, the buzz of the clippers and the careful movements of my hands, knowing more by touch than by sight. When I was young, my father used to do it, in the hallway on the top floor of our Abnegation house. He was always too careless with the blade, and scraped the back of my neck, or nicked my ear. But he never complained about having to cut my hair for me. That's something, I guess.

Nita is tapping her foot. This time she wears a white short-sleeved shirt, her hair pulled back. She smiles, but it doesn't quite reach her eyes.

"You look worried," I say.

"That's because I am," she answers. "Come on, there's a place I've been wanting to show you."

She leads me down dim hallways, empty except for the occasional janitor. They all seem to know Nita—they wave at her, or smile. She puts her hands in her pockets, guiding her eyes carefully away from mine every time we happen to look at each other.

We go through a door without a security sensor to keep it locked. The room beyond it is a wide circle with a chandelier marking its center with dangling glass. The floors are polished wood, dark, and the walls, covered in sheets of bronze, gleam where the light touches them. There are names inscribed on the bronze panels, dozens of names.

Nita stands beneath the glass chandelier and holds her arms out, wide, to encompass the room in her gesture.

"These are the Chicago family trees," she says. "Your family trees."

I move closer to one of the walls and read through the names, searching for one that looks familiar. At the end, I find one: Uriah Pedrad and Ezekiel Pedrad. Next to each name is a small "DD," and there is a dot next to Uriah's name, and it looks freshly carved. Marking him as Divergent, probably.

"Do you know where mine is?" I say.

She crosses the room and touches one of the panels.

"The generations are matrilineal. That's why Jeanine's records said Tris was 'second generation'—because her mother came from outside the city. I'm not sure how Jeanine knew that, but I guess we'll never find out."

I approach the panel that bears my name with trepidation, though I'm not sure what I have to fear from seeing my name and my parents' names carved into bronze. I see a vertical line connecting Kristin Johnson to Evelyn Johnson, and a horizontal one connecting Evelyn Johnson to Marcus Eaton. Below the two names is just one: Tobias Eaton. The small letters beside my name are "AD," and there's a dot there too, though I now know I'm not actually Divergent.

"The first letter is your faction of origin," she says, "and the second is your faction of choice. They thought that keeping track of the factions would help them trace the path of the genes."

My mother's letters: "EAF." The "F" is for "factionless," I assume.

My father's letters: "AA," with a dot.

I touch the line connecting me to them, and the line connecting Evelyn to her parents, and the line connecting them to their parents, all the way back through eight generations, counting my own. This is a map of what I've always known, that I am tied to them, bound forever to this empty inheritance no matter how far I run.

"While I appreciate you showing me this," I say, and I feel sad, and tired, "I'm not sure why it had to happen in the middle of the night."

"I thought you might want to see it. And I had something I wanted to talk to you about."

"More reassurance that my limitations don't define me?" I shake my head. "No thanks, I've had enough of that."

"No," she says. "But I'm glad you said that."

She leans against the panel, covering Evelyn's name with her shoulder. I step back, not wanting to be so close to her that I can see the ring of lighter brown around her pupils.

"That conversation I had with you last night, about genetic damage . . . it was actually a test. I wanted to see how you would react to what I said about damaged genes, so I would know whether I could trust you or not," she says. "If you accepted what I said about your limitations, the answer would have been no." She slides a little closer to me, so her shoulder covers Marcus's name too. "See, I'm not really on board with being classified as 'damaged.'"

I think of the way she spat out the explanation of the tattoo of broken glass on her back like it was poison.

My heart starts to beat harder, so I can feel my pulse in

my throat. Bitterness has replaced the good humor in her voice, and her eyes have lost their warmth. I am afraid of her, afraid of what she says—and thrilled by it too, because it means I don't have to accept that I am smaller than I once believed.

"I take it you aren't on board with it either," she says.

"No. I'm not."

"There are a lot of secrets in this place," she says. "One of them is that, to them, a GD is expendable. Another is that some of us are not just going to sit back and take it."

"What do you mean, expendable?" I say.

"The crimes they have committed against people like us are serious," Nita says. "And hidden. I can show you evidence, but that will have to come later. For now, what I can tell you is that we're working against the Bureau, for good reasons, and we want you with us."

I narrow my eyes. "Why? What is it you want from me, exactly?"

"Right now I want to offer you an opportunity to see what the world is like outside the compound."

"And what you get in return is . . . ?"

"Your protection," she says. "I'm going to a dangerous place, and I can't tell anyone else from the Bureau about it. You're an outsider, which means it's safer for me to trust you, and I know you know how to defend yourself. And if you come with me, I'll show you that evidence you want to see."

She touches her heart, lightly, as if swearing on it. My skepticism is strong, but my curiosity is stronger. It's not hard for me to believe that the Bureau would do bad things, because every government I've ever known has done bad things, even the Abnegation oligarchy, of which my father was the head. And even beyond that reasonable suspicion, I have brewing inside me the desperate hope that I am not damaged, that I am worth more than the corrected genes I pass on to any children I might have.

So I decide to go along with this. For now.

"Fine," I say.

"First," she says, "before I show you anything, you have to accept that you won't be able to tell anyone—even Tris— about what you see. Are you all right with that?"

"She's trustworthy, you know." I promised Tris I wouldn't keep secrets from her anymore. I shouldn't get into situations where I'll have to do it again. "Why can't I tell her?"

"I'm not saying she isn't trustworthy. It's just that she doesn't have the skill set we need, and we don't want to put anyone at risk that we don't have to. See, the Bureau doesn't want us to organize. If we believe we're not 'damaged,' then we're saying that everything they're doing—the experiments, the genetic alterations, all of it—is a waste of time. And no one wants to hear that their life's work is a sham."

I know all about that—it's like finding out that the factions are an artificial system, designed by scientists to keep us under control for as long as possible.

She pulls away from the wall, and then she says the only thing she could possibly say to make me agree:

"If you tell her, you would be depriving her of the choice I'm giving you now. You would force her to become a coconspirator. By keeping this from her, you would be protecting her."

I run my fingers over my name, carved into the metal panel, Tobias Eaton. These are my genes, this is my mess. I don't want to pull Tris into it.

"All right," I say. "Show me."

+ + +

I watch her flashlight beam bob up and down with her footsteps. We just retrieved a bag from a mop closet down the hall—she was ready for this. She leads me deep into the underground hallways of the compound, past the place where the GDs gather, to a corridor where the electricity no longer flows. At a certain place she crouches and slides her hand along the ground until her fingers reach a latch. She hands me the flashlight and pulls back the latch, lifting a door from the tile.

"It's an escape tunnel," she says. "They dug it when they first came here, so there would always be a way to escape during an emergency."

From her bag she takes a black tube and twists off the top. It sprays sparks of light that glow red against her skin. She releases it over the doorway and it falls several feet, leaving a streak of light on my eyelids. She sits on the edge of the hole, her backpack secure around her shoulders, and drops.

I know it's just a short way down, but it feels like more with the space open beneath me. I sit, the silhouette of my shoes dark against the red sparks, and push myself forward.

"Interesting," Nita says when I land. I lift up the flashlight, and she holds the flare out in front of her as we walk down the tunnel, which is just wide enough for the two of us to walk side by side, and just tall enough for me to straighten up. It smells rich and rotten, like mold and dead air. "I forgot you were afraid of heights."

"Well, I'm not afraid of much else," I say.

"No need to get defensive!" She smiles. "I actually have always wanted to ask you about that."

I step over a puddle, the soles of my shoes gripping the gritty tunnel floor.

"Your third fear," she says. "Shooting that woman. Who was she?"

The flare goes out, so the flashlight I'm holding is our only guide through the tunnel. I shift my arm to create more space between us, not wanting to skim her arm in the dark.

"She wasn't anyone in particular," I say. "The fear was shooting her."

"You were afraid of shooting people?"

"No," I say. "I was afraid of my considerable capacity to kill."

She is silent, and so am I. That's the first time I've ever said those words out loud, and now I hear how strange they are. How many young men fear that there is a monster inside them? People are supposed to fear others, not themselves. People are supposed to aspire to become their fathers, not shudder at the thought.

"I've always wondered what would be in my fear landscape." She says it in a hushed tone, like a prayer. "Sometimes I feel like there is so much to be afraid of, and sometimes I feel like there is nothing left to fear."

I nod, though she can't see me, and we keep moving, the flashlight beam bouncing, our shoes scraping, the moldy air rushing toward us from whatever is on the other end.

+ + +

After twenty minutes of walking, we turn a corner and I smell fresh wind, cold enough to make me shudder. I turn off the flashlight, and the moonlight at the end of the tunnel guides us to our exit.

The tunnel let us out somewhere in the wasteland we drove through to get to the compound, among the crumbling buildings and overgrown trees breaking through the pavement. Parked a few feet away is an old truck, the back covered in shredded, threadbare canvas. Nita kicks one of the tires to test it, then climbs into the driver's seat. The keys already dangle from the ignition.

"Whose truck?" I say when I get into the passenger's seat.

"It belongs to the people we're going to meet. I asked them to park it here," she says.

"And who are they?"

"Friends of mine."

I don't know how she finds her way through the maze of streets before us, but she does, steering the truck around tree roots and fallen streetlights, flashing the headlights at animals that scamper at the edge of my vision.

A long-legged creature with a brown, spare body picks

its way across the street ahead of us, almost as tall as the headlights. Nita eases on the brakes so she doesn't hit it. Its ears twitch, and its dark, round eyes watch us with careful curiosity, like a child.

"Sort of beautiful, aren't they?" she says. "Before I came here I'd never seen a deer."

I nod. It is elegant, but hesitant, halting.

Nita presses the horn with her fingertips, and the deer moves out of the way. We accelerate again, then reach a wide, open road suspended across the railroad tracks I once walked down to reach the compound. I see its lights up ahead, the one bright spot in this dark wasteland.

And we are traveling northeast, away from it.

+ + +

It is a long time before I see electric light again. When I do, it is along a narrow, patchy street. The bulbs dangle from a cord strung along the old streetlights.

"We stop here." Nita jerks the wheel, pulling the truck into an alley between two brick buildings. She takes the keys from the ignition and looks at me. "Check in the glove box. I asked them to give us weapons."

I open the compartment in front of me. Sitting on top of some old wrappers are two knives.

"How are you with a knife?" she says.

The Dauntless taught initiates how to throw knives even before the changes to initiation that Max made before I joined them. I never liked it, because it seemed like a way to encourage the Dauntless flair for theatrics, rather than a useful skill.

"I'm all right," I say with a smirk. "I never thought that skill would actually be worth anything, though."

"I guess the Dauntless are good for something after all . . . *Four*," she says, smiling a little. She takes the larger of the two knives, and I take the smaller one.

I am tense, turning the handle in my fingers as we walk down the alley. Above me the windows flicker with a different kind of light—flames, from candles or lanterns. At one point, when I glance up, I see a curtain of hair and dark eye sockets staring back at me.

"People live here," I say.

"This is the very edge of the fringe," Nita says. "It's about a two-hour drive from Milwaukee, which is a metropolitan area north of here. Yeah, people live here. These days people don't venture too far away from cities, even if they want to live outside the government's influence, like the people here."

"Why do they want to live outside the government's influence?" I know what living outside the government is like, by watching the factionless. They were always

"What is it." I laugh. "Let me put it this way: I just found out you're not the worst person I know."

I drop into a crouch and push my fingers through my hair. I feel numb and terrified of my own numbness. The Bureau is responsible for my parents' deaths. Why do I have to keep repeating it to myself to believe it? What's wrong with me?

"Oh," he says. "I'm . . . sorry?"

All I can manage is a small grunt.

"You know what Mom told me once?" he says, and the way he says *Mom*, like he didn't *betray* her, sets my teeth on edge. "She said that everyone has some evil inside them, and the first step to loving anyone is to recognize the same evil in ourselves, so we're able to forgive them."

"Is that what you want me to do?" I say dully as I stand. "I may have done bad things, Caleb, but I would *never* deliver you to your own execution."

"You can't say that," he says, and it sounds like he's pleading with me, begging me to say that I am just like him, no better. "You didn't know how persuasive Jeanine was—"

Something inside me snaps like a brittle rubber band.

I punch him in the face.

All I can think about is how the Erudite stripped me of my watch and my shoes and led me to the bare table where they would take my life. A table that Caleb may as well have set up himself.

I thought I was beyond this kind of anger, but as he stumbles back with his hands on his face, I pursue him, grabbing the front of his shirt and slamming him against the stone sculpture and screaming that he is a coward and a traitor and that I will kill him, I will kill him.

One of the guards comes toward me, and all she has to do is put her hand on my arm and the spell is broken. I release Caleb's shirt. I shake out my stinging hand. I turn and walk away.

+ + +

There's a beige sweater draped over the empty chair in Matthew's lab, the sleeve brushing the floor. I've never met his supervisor. I'm beginning to suspect that Matthew does all the real work.

I sit on top of the sweater and examine my knuckles. A few of them are split from punching Caleb, and dotted with faint bruises. It seems fitting that the blow would leave a mark on both of us. That's how the world works.

Last night, when I went back to the dormitory, Tobias wasn't there, and I was too angry to sleep. In the hours that I lay awake, staring at the ceiling, I decided that while I wasn't going to participate in Nita's plan, I also wasn't going to stop it. The truth about the attack simulation brewed hate for the Bureau inside me, and I want to watch it break apart from within.

Matthew is talking science. I'm having trouble paying attention.

"—doing some genetic analysis, which is fine, but before, we were developing a way to make the memory compound behave as a virus," he says. "With the same rapid replication, the same ability to spread through the air. And then we developed a vaccination for it. Just a temporary one, only lasts for forty-eight hours, but still."

I nod. "So . . . you were making it so you could set up other city experiments more efficiently, right?" I say. "No need to inject everyone with the memory serum when you can just release it and let it spread."

"Exactly!" He seems excited that I'm actually interested in what he's saying. "And it's a better model for having the option to select particular members of a population to opt out—you inoculate them, the virus spreads within twenty-four hours, and it has no effect on them."

I nod again.

"You okay?" Matthew says, his coffee mug poised near his mouth. He puts it down. "I heard the security guards had to pull you off someone last night."

"It was my brother. Caleb."

"Ah." Matthew raises an eyebrow. "What did he do this time?"

"Nothing, really." I pinch the sweater sleeve between my fingers. Its edges are all fraying, wearing with time. "I was wired to explode anyway; he just got in the way."

I already know, by looking at him, the question he's asking, and I want to explain it all to him, everything that Nita showed me and told me. I wonder if I can trust him.

"I heard something yesterday," I say, testing the waters. "About the Bureau. About my city, and the simulations."

He straightens up and gives me a strange look.

"What?" I say.

"Did you hear that something from Nita?" he says.

"Yes. How did you know that?"

"I've helped her a couple times," he says. "I let her into that storage room. Did she tell you anything else?"

Matthew is Nita's informant? I stare at him. I never thought that Matthew, who went out of his way to show me the difference between my "pure" genes and Tobias's "damaged" genes, might be helping Nita.

"Something about a plan," I say slowly.

He gets up and walks toward me, oddly tense. I lean away from him by instinct.

"Is it happening?" he says. "Do you know when?"

"What's going on?" I say. "Why would you help Nita?"

"Because all this 'genetic damage' nonsense is ridiculous," he says. "It's very important that you answer my questions."

"It is happening. And I don't know when, but I think it will be soon."

"Shit." Matthew puts his hands on his face. "Nothing good can come of this."

"If you don't stop saying cryptic things, I'm going to slap you," I say, getting to my feet.

"I was helping Nita until she told me what she and those fringe people wanted to do," Matthew says. "They want to get to the Weapons Lab and—"

"—steal the memory serum, yeah, I heard."

"No." He shakes his head. "No, they don't want the memory serum, they want the death serum. Similar to the one the Erudite have—the one you were supposed to be injected with when you were almost executed. They're going to use it for assassinations, a lot of them. Set off an aerosol can and it's easy, see? Give it to the right people and you have an explosion of anarchy and violence, which is exactly what those fringe people want."

I do see. I see the tilt of a vial, the quick press of a button on an aerosol can. I see Abnegation bodies and Erudite bodies sprawled over streets and staircases. I see the little pieces of this world that we've managed to cling to bursting into flames.

"I thought I was helping her with something smarter," Matthew says. "If I had known I was helping her start another war, I wouldn't have done it. We have to do something about this."

"I told him," I say softly, but not to Matthew, to myself. "I told him she was lying."

"We may have a problem with the way we treat GDs in this country, but it's not going to be solved by killing a bunch of people," he says. "Now come on, we're going to David's office."

I don't know what's right or wrong. I don't know anything about this country or the way it works or what it needs to change. But I do know that a bunch of death serum in the hands of Nita and some people from the fringe is no better than a bunch of death serum in the Weapons Lab of the Bureau. So I chase Matthew down the hallway outside. We walk quickly in the direction of the front entrance, where I first entered this compound.

When we walk past the security checkpoint, I spot Uriah near the sculpture. He lifts a hand to wave to me, his mouth pressed into a line that could be a smile if he was trying harder. Above his head, light refracts through the water tank, the symbol of the compound's slow, pointless struggle.

I'm just passing the security checkpoint when I see the

wall next to Uriah explode.

It is like fire blossoming from a bud. Shards of glass and metal spray from the center of the bloom, and Uriah's body is among them, a limp projectile. A deep rumble moves through me like a shudder. My mouth is open; I am screaming his name, but I can't hear myself over the ringing in my ears.

Around me, everyone is crouched, their arms curled around their heads. But I am on my feet, watching the hole in the compound wall. No one comes through it.

Seconds later, everyone around me starts running away from the blast, and I hurl myself against them, shoulder first, toward Uriah. An elbow hits me in the side and I fall down, my face scraping something hard and metal—the side of a table. I struggle to my feet, wiping blood from my eyebrow with a sleeve. Fabric slides over my arms, and limbs, hair, and wide eyes are all I can see, except the sign over their heads that says COMPOUND EXIT.

"Signal the alarms!" one of the guards at the security checkpoint screams. I duck under an arm and trip to the side.

"I did!" another guard shouts. "They aren't working!"

Matthew grabs my shoulder and yells into my ear. "What are you doing? Don't go *toward*—"

I move faster, finding an empty channel where there

are no people to obstruct my path. Matthew runs after me.

"We shouldn't be going to the explosion site—whoever set it off is already in the building," he says. "Weapons Lab, now! Come on!"

The Weapons Lab. Holy words.

I think of Uriah lying on the tile surrounded by glass and metal. My body is straining toward him, every muscle, but I know there's nothing I can do for him right now. The more important thing for me to do is to use my knowledge of chaos, of attacks, to keep Nita and her friends from stealing the death serum.

Matthew was right. Nothing good can come of this.

Matthew takes the lead, plunging into the crowd like it is a pool of water. I try to look only at the back of his head, to keep track of him, but the oncoming faces distract me, the mouths and eyes rigid with terror. I lose him for a few seconds and then find him again, several yards ahead, turning right at the next hallway.

"Matthew!" I shout, and I push my way through another group of people. Finally I catch up, grabbing the back of his shirt. He turns and grabs my hand.

"Are you okay?" he says, staring just above my eyebrow. In the rush I almost forgot about my cut. I press my sleeve to it, and it comes away red, but I nod.

"I'm fine! Let's go!"

We sprint side by side down the hallway—this one is not as crowded as the others, but I can see that whoever infiltrated the building has been here already. There are guards lying on the floor, some alive and some not. I see a gun on the tile near a drinking fountain and lurch toward it, breaking my grip on Matthew's hand.

I grab the gun and offer it to Matthew. He shakes his head. "I've never fired one."

"Oh, for God's sake." My finger curls around the trigger. It's different from the guns we had in the city—it doesn't have a barrel that shifts to the side, or the same tension in the trigger, or even the same distribution of weight. It's easier to hold, as a result, because it doesn't spark the same memories.

Matthew is gasping for air. So am I, only I don't notice it the same way, because I've done this sprint through chaos so many times. The next hallway he guides us to is empty except for one fallen soldier. She's not moving.

"It's not far," he says, and I touch my finger to my lips to tell him to be quiet.

We slow to a walk, and I squeeze the gun, my sweat making it slip. I don't know how many bullets are in it, or how to check. When we pass the soldier, I pause to search her for a weapon. I find a gun tucked under her hip, where she fell on her own wrist. Matthew stares at her, unblinking, as I take her weapon.

"Hey," I say quietly. "Just keep moving. Move now, process later."

I elbow him and lead the way down the hallway. Here the hallways are dim, the ceilings crossed with bars and pipes. I can hear people ahead and don't need Matthew's whispered directions to find them.

When we reach the place where we're supposed to turn, I press against the wall and look around the corner, careful to keep myself as hidden as possible.

There's a set of double-walled glass doors that look as heavy as metal doors would be, but they're open. Beyond them is a cramped hallway, empty except for three people in black. They wear heavy clothing and carry guns so big I'm not sure I would be able to lift one. Their faces are covered with dark fabric, disguising all but their eyes.

On his knees before the double doors is David, a gun barrel pressed to his temple, blood trailing down his chin. And standing among the invaders, wearing the same mask as the others, is a girl with a dark ponytail.

Nita.

CHAPTER
TWENTY-SEVEN

TRIS

"GET US IN, David," Nita says, her voice garbled by the mask.

David's eyes slide lazily to the side, to the man pointing the gun at him.

"I don't believe you'll shoot me," he says. "Because I'm the only one in this building who knows this information, and you want that serum."

"Won't shoot you in the head, maybe," the man says, "but there are other places."

The man and Nita exchange a look. Then the man shifts the gun down, to David's feet, and fires. I squeeze my eyes shut as David's screams fill the hallway. He might be one of the people who offered Jeanine Matthews the attack simulation, but I still don't relish his screams of pain.

I stare at the guns I carry, one in each hand, my fingers pale against the black triggers. I imagine myself trimming back all the stray branches of my thoughts, focusing on just this place, just this time.

I put my mouth right next to Matthew's ear and mutter, "Go for help. Now."

Matthew nods and starts down the hallway. To his credit, he moves quietly, his footsteps silent on the tile. At the end of the hallway he looks back at me, and then disappears around the bend.

"I'm sick of this shit," the red-haired woman says. "Just blow up the doors."

"An explosion would activate one of the backup security measures," says Nita. "We need the pass code."

I look around the corner again, and this time, David's eyes shift to mine. His face is pale and shiny with sweat, and there is a wide pool of blood around his ankles. The others are looking at Nita, who takes a black box from her pocket and opens it to reveal a syringe and needle.

"Thought you said that stuff doesn't work on him," the man with the gun says.

"I said he could *resist* it, not that it didn't work at all," she says. "David, this is a very potent blend of truth serum and fear serum. I'm going to stick you with it if you don't tell us the pass code."

"I know this is just the fault of your genes, Nita," David

says weakly. "If you stop now, I can help you, I can—"

Nita smiles a twisted smile. With relish, she sticks the needle in his neck and presses the plunger. David slumps over, and then his body shudders, and shudders again.

He opens his eyes wide and screams, staring at the empty air, and I know what he's seeing, because I've seen it myself, in Erudite headquarters, under the influence of the terror serum. I watched my worst fears come to life.

Nita kneels in front of him and grabs his face.

"David!" she says urgently. "I can make it stop if you tell us how to get into this room. Hear me?"

He pants, and his eyes aren't focused on her, but rather on something over her shoulder. "Don't do it!" he shouts, and he lunges forward, toward whatever phantom the serum is showing him. Nita puts an arm across his chest to keep him steady, and he screams, "Don't—!"

Nita shakes him. "I'll stop them from doing it if you tell me how to get in!"

"Her!" David says, and tears gleam in his eyes. "The— the name—"

"Whose name?"

"We're running out of time!" the man with the gun trained on David says. "Either we get the serum or we kill him—"

"Her," David says, pointing at the space in front of him. Pointing at me.

I stretch my arms around the corner of the wall and fire twice. The first bullet hits the wall. The second hits the man in the arm, so the huge weapon topples to the floor. The red-haired woman points her weapon at me—or the part of me that she can see, half hidden by the wall—and Nita screams, "Hold your fire!"

"Tris," Nita says, "you don't know what you're doing—"

"You're probably right," I say, and I fire again. This time my hand is steadier, my aim is better; I hit Nita's side, right above her hip. She screams into her mask and clutches the hole in her skin, sinking to her knees, her hands covered in blood.

David surges toward me with a grimace of pain as he puts weight on his injured leg. I wrap my arm around his waist and swing his body around so he's between me and the remaining soldiers. Then I press one of my guns to the back of his head.

They all freeze. I can feel my heartbeat in my throat, in my hands, behind my eyes.

"Fire, and I'll shoot him in the head," I say.

"You wouldn't kill your own leader," the red-haired woman says.

"He's not my leader. I don't care if he lives or dies," I say. "But if you think I'm going to let you gain control of that death serum, you're insane."

I start to shuffle backward, with David whimpering in

front of me, still under the influence of the serum cocktail. I duck my head and turn my body sideways so it's safely behind his. I keep one of the guns against his head.

We reach the end of the hallway, and the woman calls my bluff. She fires, and hits David just above the knee, in his other leg. He collapses with a scream, and I am exposed. I dive to the ground, slamming my elbows into the floor, as a bullet goes past me, the sound vibrating inside my head.

Then I feel something hot spreading through my left arm, and I see blood and my feet scramble on the floor, searching for traction. I find it and fire blindly down the hallway. I grab David by the collar and drag him around the corner, pain searing through my left arm.

I hear running footsteps and groan. But they aren't coming from behind me; they're coming from in front. People surround me, Matthew among them, and some of them pick David up and run with him down the hallway. Matthew offers me his hand.

My ears are ringing. I can't believe I did it.

CHAPTER
TWENTY-EIGHT

TRIS

THE HOSPITAL IS packed with people, all of them yelling or racing back and forth or yanking curtains shut. Before I sat down I checked all the beds for Tobias. He wasn't in any of them. I am still shaking with relief.

Uriah is not here either. He is in one of the other rooms, and the door is closed—not a good sign.

The nurse who dabs my arm with antiseptic is breathless and looks around at all the activity instead of at my wound. I'm told it's a minor graze, nothing to worry about.

"I can wait, if you need to do something else," I say. "I have to find someone anyway."

She purses her lips, then says, "You need stitches."

"It's just a graze!"

"Not your arm, your head," she says, pointing to a spot above my eye. I had almost forgotten about the cut in all the chaos, but it still hasn't stopped bleeding.

"Fine."

"I'm going to have to give you a shot of this numbing agent," she says, holding up a syringe.

I am so used to needles that I don't even react. She dabs my forehead with antiseptic—they are so careful about germs here—and I feel the sting and prickle of the needle, diminishing by the second as the numbing agent does its work.

I watch the people rush past as she stitches my skin—a doctor pulls off a pair of bloodstained rubber gloves; a nurse carries a tray of gauze, his shoes nearly slipping on the tile; a family member of someone injured wrings her hands. The air smells like chemicals and old paper and warm bodies.

"Any updates on David?" I say.

"He'll live, but it will take him a long time to walk again," she says. Her lips stop puckering, just for a few seconds. "Could have been a lot worse, if you hadn't been there. You're all set."

I nod. I wish I could tell her that I'm not a hero, that I was using him as a shield, like a wall of meat. I wish I could confess to being a person full of hate for the Bureau and for David, a person who would let someone else get riddled with bullets to save herself. My parents would be ashamed.

She places a bandage over the stitches to protect the wound, and gathers all the wrappers and soaked cotton balls into her fists to throw them away.

Before I can thank her, she is gone, off to the next bed, the next patient, the next injury.

Injured people line the hallway outside the emergency ward. I have gathered from the evidence that there was another explosion set off at the same time as the one near the entrance. Both were diversions. Our attackers got in through the underground tunnel, as Nita said they would. She never mentioned blowing holes in walls.

The doors at the end of the hallway open, and a few people rush in, carrying a young woman—Nita—between them. They put her on a cot near one of the walls. She groans, clutching at a roll of gauze that is pressed to the wound in her side. I feel strangely separate from her pain. I shot her. I had to. That's the end of it.

As I walk down the aisle between the wounded, I notice the uniforms. Everyone sitting here wears green. With few exceptions, they are all support staff. They are clutching bleeding arms or legs or heads, their injuries no better than my own, some much worse.

I catch my reflection in the windows just beyond the main corridor—my hair is stringy and limp, and the bandage dominates my forehead. David's blood and my blood smear my clothes in places. I need to shower and change, but first I have to find Tobias and Christina. I haven't seen either of them since before the invasion.

It doesn't take me long to find Christina—she is sitting in the waiting room when I walk out of the emergency ward, her knee jiggling so much that the person next to her is giving her dirty looks. She lifts a hand to greet me, but her eyes shift away from mine and toward the doors right afterward.

"You all right?" she asks me.

"Yeah," I say. "There's still no update on Uriah. I couldn't get into the room."

"These people make me crazy, you know that?" she says. "They won't tell anyone anything. They won't let us see him. It's like they think they own him and everything that happens to him!"

"They work differently here. I'm sure they'll tell you when they know something concrete."

"Well, they would tell *you*," she says, scowling. "But I'm not convinced they would give *me* a second look."

A few days ago I might have disagreed with her, unsure how influential their belief in genetic damage was on their behavior. I'm not sure what to do—not sure how to talk to her now that I have these advantages and she does not and there's nothing either of us can do about it. All I can think to do is be near her.

"I have to find Tobias, but I'll come back after I do and sit with you, okay?"

She finally looks at me, and her knee goes still. "They didn't tell you?"

My stomach clenches with fear. "Tell me what."

"Tobias was arrested," she says quietly. "I saw him sitting with the invaders right before I came in here. Some people saw him at the control room before the attack—they say he was disabling the alarm system."

There is a sad look in her eyes, like she pities me. But I already knew what Tobias did.

"Where are they?" I say.

I need to talk to him. And I know what I need to say.

CHAPTER TWENTY-NINE

TOBIAS

MY WRISTS STING from the plastic tie the guard squeezed around them. I probe my jaw with just my fingertips, testing the skin for blood.

"All right?" Reggie says.

I nod. I have dealt with worse injuries than this—I have been hit harder than I was by the soldier who slammed the butt of his gun into my jaw while he was arresting me. His eyes were wild with anger when he did it.

Mary and Rafi sit a few feet away, Rafi clutching a handful of gauze to his bleeding arm. A guard stands between us and them, keeping us separate. As I look at them, Rafi meets my eyes and nods. As if to say, *Well done.*

If I did well, why do I feel sick to my stomach?

"Listen," Reggie says, shifting so he's closer to me. "Nita and the fringe people are taking the fall. It'll be all right."

I nod again, without conviction. We had a backup plan for our probable arrest, and I'm not worried about its success. What I am worried about is how long it's taking them to deal with us, and how casual it has been—we have been sitting against a wall in an empty corridor since they caught the invaders more than an hour ago, and no one has come to tell us what will happen to us, or to ask us any questions. I haven't even seen Nita yet.

It puts a sour taste in my mouth. Whatever we did, it seems to have shaken them up, and I know of nothing that shakes people up as much as lost lives.

How many of those am I responsible for, because I participated in this?

"Nita told me they were going to steal memory serum," I say to Reggie, and I'm afraid to look at him. "Was that true?"

Reggie eyes the guard who stands a few feet away. We have already been yelled at once for talking.

But I know the answer.

"It wasn't, was it," I say. Tris was right. Nita was lying.

"Hey!" The guard marches toward us and sticks the barrel of her gun between us. "Move aside. No conversation allowed."

Reggie shifts to the right, and I make eye contact with the guard.

"What's going on?" I say. "What happened?"

"Oh, like you don't know," she answers. "Now keep your mouth shut."

I watch her walk away, and then I see a small blond girl appear at the end of the hallway. Tris. A bandage stretches across her forehead, and blood smears her clothes in the shape of fingers. She clutches a piece of paper in her fist.

"Hey!" the guard says. "What are you doing here?"

"Shelly," the other guard says, jogging over. "Calm down. That's the girl who saved David."

The girl who saved David—from what, exactly?

"Oh." Shelly puts her gun down. "Well, it's still a valid question."

"They asked me to bring you guys an update," Tris says, and she offers Shelly the piece of paper. "David is in recovery. He'll live, but they're not sure when he'll walk again. Most of the other injured have been cared for."

The sour taste in my mouth grows stronger. David can't walk. And what they've been doing all this time is caring for the injured. All this destruction, and for what? I don't even know. I don't know the truth.

What did I do?

"Do they have a casualty count?" Shelly asks.

"Not yet," Tris replies.

"Thanks for letting us know."

"Listen." She shifts her weight to one foot. "I need to talk to him."

She jerks her head toward me.

"We can't really—" Shelly starts.

"Just for a second, I promise," Tris says. "Please."

"Let her," the other guard says. "What could it hurt?"

"Fine," Shelly says. "I'll give you two minutes."

She nods to me, and I use the wall to push myself to my feet, my hands still bound in front of me. Tris comes closer, but not that close—the space, and her folded arms, form a barrier between us that may as well be a wall. She looks somewhere south of my eyes.

"Tris, I—"

"Want to know what your friends did?" she says. Her voice shakes, and I do not make the mistake of thinking it's from tears. It's from anger. "They weren't after the memory serum. They were after poison—death serum. So that they could kill a bunch of important government people and start a war."

I look down, at my hands, at the tile, at the toes of her shoes. A war. "I didn't know—"

"I was right. I was right, and you didn't listen. Again," she says, quiet. Her eyes lock on mine, and I find that I do not want the eye contact I craved, because it takes me apart, piece by piece. "Uriah was standing right in front of one of the explosives they set off as diversions. He's unconscious and they're not sure he'll wake up."

It's strange how a word, a phrase, a sentence, can feel like a blow to the head.

"What?"

All I can see is Uriah's face when he hit the net after the Choosing Ceremony, the giddy smile he wore as Zeke and I pulled him onto the platform next to the net. Or him sitting in the tattoo parlor, his ear taped forward so it wouldn't get in Tori's way as she drew a snake on his skin. Uriah might not wake up? Uriah, gone forever?

And I promised. I promised Zeke I would look after him, I *promised* . . .

"He's one of the last friends I have," she says, her voice breaking. "I don't know if I'll ever be able to look at you the same way again."

She walks away. I hear Shelly's muffled voice telling me to sit down, and I sink to my knees, letting my wrists rest on my legs. I struggle to find a way to escape this, the horror of what I've done, but there is no sophisticated logic that can liberate me; there is no way out.

I put my face in my hands and try not to think, try not to imagine anything at all.

+ + +

"That's not necessarily true," Matthew says, pinching the string around his neck and then twisting it. "We don't see that many Divergent resisting truth serum. Just Tris, in recent memory. The capacity for serum resistance seems to be higher in some people than others—take yourself, for example, Tobias." Matthew shrugs. "Still, this is why I invited *you*, Caleb. You've worked on the serums before. You might know them as well as I do. Maybe we can develop a truth serum that is more difficult to resist."

"I don't want to do that kind of work anymore," Caleb says.

"Oh, shut—" starts Tris, but Matthew interrupts her.

"Please, Caleb," he says.

Caleb and Tris exchange a look. The skin on his face and on her knuckles is nearly the same color, purple-blue-green, as if drawn with ink. This is what happens when siblings collide—they injure each other the same way. Caleb sinks back against the countertop edge, touching the back of his head to the metal cabinets.

"Fine," Caleb says. "As long as you promise not to use this against me, Beatrice."

"Why would I?" Tris says.

"I can help," Cara says, lifting a hand. "I've worked on serums too, as an Erudite."

"Great." Matthew claps his hands together. "Meanwhile, Tris will be playing the spy."

"What about me?" Christina says.

"I was hoping you and Tobias could get in with Reggie," Tris says. "David wouldn't tell me about the backup security measures in the Weapons Lab, but Nita can't have been the only one who knew about them."

"You want me to get *in* with the guy who set off the explosives that put Uriah in a coma?" Christina says.

"You don't have to be friends," Tris says, "you just need to talk to him about what he knows. Tobias can help you."

"I don't need Four; I can do it myself," Christina says.

She shifts on the exam table, tearing the paper beneath her with her thigh, and gives me another sour look. I know it must be Uriah's blank face she sees when she looks at me. I feel like there is something stuck in my throat.

"You do need me, actually, because he already trusts me," I say. "And those people are very secretive, which means this will require subtlety."

"I can be subtle," Christina says.

"No, you can't."

"He's got a *point* . . ." Tris sings with a smile.

Christina smacks her arm, and Tris smacks her back.

"It's all settled, then," Matthew says. "I think we should meet again after Tris has been to the council meeting, which is on Friday. Come here at five."

He approaches Cara and Caleb and says something

about chemical compounds I don't quite understand. Christina walks out, bumping me with her shoulder as she leaves. Tris lifts her eyes to mine.

"We should talk," I say.

"Fine," she says, and I follow her into the hallway.

We stand next to the door until everyone else leaves. Her shoulders are drawn in like she's trying to make herself even smaller, trying to evaporate on the spot, and we stand too far apart, the entire width of the hallway between us. I try to remember the last time I kissed her and I can't.

Finally we're alone, and the hallway is quiet. My hands start to tingle and go numb, the way they always do when I panic.

"Do you think you'll ever forgive me?" I say.

She shakes her head, but says, "I don't know. I think that's what I need to figure out."

"You know . . . you *know* I never wanted Uriah to get hurt, right?" I look at the stitches crossing her forehead and I add, "Or you. I never wanted you to get hurt either."

She's tapping her foot, her body shifting with the movement. She nods. "I know that."

"I had to do something," I say. "I *had* to."

"A lot of people got hurt," she says. "All because you dismissed what I said, because—and this is the worst part, Tobias—because you thought I was being petty and *jealous*. Just some silly sixteen-year-old girl, right?" She shakes her head.

"I would never call you silly or petty," I say sternly. "I thought your judgment was clouded, yes. But that's all."

"That's enough." Her fingers slide through her hair and wrap around it. "It's just the same thing all over again, isn't it? You don't respect me as much as you say you do. When it comes down to it, you still believe I can't think rationally—"

"That is *not* what's happening!" I say hotly. "I respect you more than anyone. But right now I'm wondering what bothers you more, that I made a stupid decision or that I didn't make *your* decision."

"What's that supposed to mean?"

"It means," I say, "that you may have said you just wanted us to be honest with each other, but I think you really wanted me to always agree with you."

"I can't believe you would say that! You were *wrong*—"

"Yeah, I was wrong!" I'm shouting now, and I don't know where the anger came from, except that I can feel it swirling around inside me, violent and vicious and the strongest I have felt in days. "I was wrong, I made a huge mistake! My best friend's brother is as good as dead! And now you're acting like a parent, punishing me for it because I didn't do as I was told. Well, you are not my parent, Tris, and you don't get to tell me what to do, what to choose—!"

"Stop yelling at me," she says quietly, and she finally looks at me. I used to see all kinds of things in her eyes, love and longing and curiosity, but now all I see is anger. "Just stop."

Her quiet voice stalls the anger inside me, and I relax into the wall behind me, shoving my hands into my pockets. I didn't mean to yell at her. I didn't mean to get angry at all.

I stare, shocked, as tears touch her cheeks. I haven't seen her cry in a long time. She sniffs, and gulps, and tries to sound normal, but she doesn't.

"I just need some time," she says, choking on each word. "Okay?"

"Okay," I say.

She wipes her cheeks with her palms and walks down the hallway. I watch her blond head until it disappears around the bend, and I feel bare, like there's nothing left to protect me against pain. Her absence stings worst of all.

CHAPTER
THIRTY-FOUR

TRIS

"THERE SHE IS," Amar says as I approach the group. "Here, I'll get you your vest, Tris."

"My . . . vest?" As promised by David yesterday, I'm going to the fringe this afternoon. I don't know what to expect, which usually makes me nervous, but I'm too worn-out from the past few days to feel much of anything.

"Bulletproof vest. The fringe is not all that safe," he says, and he reaches into a crate near the doors, sorting through a stack of thick black vests to find the right size. He emerges with one that still looks far too big for me. "Sorry, not much variety here. This will work just fine. Arms up."

He guides me into the vest and tightens the straps at my sides.

"I didn't know you would be here," I say.

"Well, what did you think I did at the Bureau? Just wandered around cracking jokes?" He smiles. "They found a good use for my Dauntless expertise. I'm part of the security team. So is George. We usually just handle compound security, but any time anyone wants to go to the fringe, I volunteer."

"Talking about me?" George, who was standing in the group by the doors. "Hi, Tris. I hope he's not saying anything bad."

George puts his arm across Amar's shoulders, and they grin at each other. George looks better than the last time I saw him, but grief leaves its mark on his expression, taking the crinkles out of the corners of his eyes when he smiles, taking the dimple from his cheek.

"I was thinking we should give her a gun," Amar says. He glances at me. "We don't normally give potential future council members weapons, because they have no clue how to use them, but it's pretty clear that you do."

"It's really all right," I say. "I don't need—"

"No, you're probably a better shot than most of them," George says. "We could use another Dauntless on board with us. Let me go get one."

A few minutes later I am armed and walking with Amar to the truck. He and I get in the far back, George and a woman named Ann get in the middle, and two older security officers named Jack and Violet get in the front. The back of the truck is covered with a hard black material. The back doors look opaque and black from the outside, but from the inside they're transparent, so we can see where we're going. I am nestled between Amar and stacks of equipment that block our view of the front of the truck. George peers over the equipment and grins when the truck starts, but other than that, it's just Amar and me.

I watch the compound disappear behind us. We drive through the gardens and outbuildings that surround it, and peeking out from behind the edge of the compound are the airplanes, white and stationary. We reach the fence, and the gates open for us. I hear Jack speaking to the soldier at the outer fence, telling him our plans and the contents of the vehicle—a series of words I don't understand—before we can be released into the wild.

I ask, "What's the purpose of this patrol? Beyond showing me how things work, I mean."

"We've always kept an eye on the fringe, which is the nearest genetically damaged area outside the compound. Mostly just research, studying how the genetically damaged behave," Amar says. "But after the attack, David and the council decided we needed more extensive surveillance set up there so we can prevent an attack from happening again."

We drive past the same kind of ruins I saw when we left the city—the buildings collapsing under their own weight, and the plants roaming wild over the land, breaking through concrete.

I don't know Amar, and I don't exactly trust him, but I have to ask:

"So you believe it all? All the stuff about genetic damage being the cause of . . . *this*?"

All his old friends in the experiment were GDs. Can he possibly believe that they're damaged, that there's something wrong with them?

"You don't?" Amar says. "The way I see it, the earth has been around for a long, long time. Longer than we can imagine. And before the Purity War, no one had ever done *this*, right?" He waves his hand to indicate the world outside.

"I don't know," I say. "I find it hard to believe that they didn't."

"Such a grim view of human nature you have," he says.

I don't respond.

He continues, "Anyway, if something like that had happened in our history, the Bureau would know about it."

That strikes me as naive, for someone who once lived in my city and saw, at least on the screens, how many secrets we kept from one another. Evelyn tried to control people by controlling weapons, but Jeanine was more ambitious—she knew that when you control information, or manipulate it, you don't need force to keep people under your thumb. They stay there willingly.

That is what the Bureau—and the entire government, probably—is doing: conditioning people to be happy under its thumb.

We ride in silence for a while, with just the sound of jiggling equipment and the engine to accompany us. At first I look at every building we pass, wondering what it once housed, and then they start to blend together for me. How many different kinds of ruin do you have to see before you resign yourself to calling it all "ruin"?

"We're almost at the fringe," George calls from the middle of the truck. "We're going to stop here and advance on foot. Everyone take some equipment and set it up—except Amar, who should just look after Tris. Tris, you're welcome to get out and have a look, but stay with Amar."

I feel like all my nerves are too close to the surface, and the slightest touch will make them fire. The fringe is where my mother retreated after witnessing a murder—it is where the Bureau found her and rescued her because they suspected her genetic code was sound. Now I will walk there, to the place where, in some ways, it all began.

The truck stops, and Amar shoves the doors open. He

holds his gun in one hand and beckons to me with the other. I jump out behind him.

There are buildings here, but they are not nearly as prominent as the makeshift homes, made of scrap metal and plastic tarps, piled up right next to one another like they are holding one another upright. In the narrow aisles between them are people, mostly children, selling things from trays, or carrying buckets of water, or cooking over open fires.

When the ones nearest to us see us, a young boy takes off running and screams, "Raid! Raid!"

"Don't worry about that," Amar says to me. "They think we're soldiers. Sometimes they raid to transport the kids to orphanages."

I barely acknowledge the comment. Instead I start walking down one of the aisles, as most people take off or shut themselves inside their lean-tos with cardboard or more tarp. I see them through the cracks between the walls, their houses not much more than a pile of food and supplies on one side and sleeping mats on the other. I wonder what they do in the winter. Or what they do for a toilet.

I think of the flowers inside the compound, and the wood floors, and all the beds in the hotel that are unoccupied, and say, "Do you ever help them?"

"We believe that the best way to help our world is to fix its genetic deficiencies," Amar says, like he's reciting it from memory. "Feeding people is just putting a tiny bandage on a gaping wound. It might stop the bleeding for a while, but ultimately the wound will still be there."

I can't respond. All I do is shake my head a little and keep walking. I am beginning to understand why my mother joined Abnegation when she was supposed to join Erudite. If she had really craved safety from Erudite's growing corruption, she could have gone to Amity or Candor. But she chose the faction where she could help the helpless, and dedicated most of her life to making sure the factionless were provided for.

They must have reminded her of this place, of the fringe.

I turn my head away from Amar so he won't see the tears in my eyes. "Let's go back to the truck."

"You all right?"

"Yeah."

We both turn around to head back to the truck, but then we hear gunshots.

And right after them, a shout. "Help!"

Everyone around us scatters.

"That's George," Amar says, and he takes off running down one of the aisles on our right. I chase him into the scrap-metal structures, but he's too quick for me, and this place is a maze—I lose him in seconds, and then I am alone.

As much automatic, Abnegation-bred sympathy as I have for the people living in this place, I am also afraid of them. If they are like the factionless, then they are surely desperate like the factionless, and I am wary of desperate people.

A hand closes around my arm and drags me backward, into one of the aluminum lean-tos. Inside everything is tinted blue from the tarp that covers the walls, insulating the structure against the cold. The floor is covered with plywood, and standing in front of me is a small, thin woman with a grubby face.

"You don't want to be out there," she says. "They'll lash out at anyone, no matter how young she is."

"They?" I say.

"Lots of angry people here in the fringe," the woman says. "Some people's anger makes them want to kill everyone they perceive as an enemy. Some people's makes them more constructive."

"Well, thank you for the help," I say. "My name is Tris."

"Amy. Sit."

"I can't," I say. "My friends are out there."

"Then you should wait until the hordes of people run

to wherever your friends are, and then sneak up on them from behind."

That sounds smart.

I sink to the floor, my gun digging into my leg. The bulletproof vest is so stiff it's hard to get comfortable, but I do the best I can to seem relaxed. I hear people running outside and shouting. Amy flicks the corner of the tarp back to see outside.

"So you and your friends aren't soldiers," Amy says, still looking outside. "Which means you must be Genetic Welfare types, right?"

"No," I say. "I mean, they are, but I'm from the city. I mean, Chicago."

Amy's eyebrows pop up high. "Damn. Has it been disbanded?"

"Not yet."

"That's unfortunate."

"Unfortunate?" I frown at her. "That's my home you're talking about, you know."

"Well your home is perpetuating the belief that genetically damaged people need to be fixed—that they're *damaged*, period, which they—we—are not. So yes, it's unfortunate that the experiments still exist. I won't apologize for saying so."

I hadn't thought about it that way. To me Chicago has

to keep existing because the people I have lost lived there, because the way of life I once loved continues there, though in a broken form. But I didn't realize that Chicago's very existence could be harmful to people outside who just want to be thought of as whole.

"It's time for you to go," Amy says, dropping the corner of the tarp. "They're probably in one of the meeting areas, northwest of here."

"Thank you again," I say.

She nods to me, and I duck out of her makeshift home, the boards creaking beneath my feet.

I move through the aisles, fast, glad that all the people scattered when we arrived so there is no one to block my way. I jump over a puddle of—well, I don't want to know what it is—and emerge into a kind of courtyard, where a tall, gangly boy has a gun pointed at George.

A small crowd of people surrounds the boy with the gun. They have distributed among them the surveillance equipment George was carrying, and they're destroying it, hitting it with shoes or rocks or hammers.

George's eyes shift to me, but I touch a finger to my lips, hastily. I am behind the crowd now; the one with the gun doesn't know I'm there.

"Put the gun down," George says.

"No!" the boy answers. His pale eyes keep shifting

from George to the people around him and back. "Went to a lot of trouble to get this, not gonna give it to you now."

"Then just . . . let me go. You can keep it."

"Not until you tell us where you've been taking our people!" the boy says.

"We haven't taken any of your people," George says. "We're not soldiers. We're just scientists."

"Yeah, right," the boy says. "A bulletproof vest? If that's not soldier shit, then I'm the richest kid in the States. Now tell me what I need to know!"

I move back so I'm standing behind one of the lean-tos, then put my gun around the edge of the structure and say, "Hey!"

Everyone in the crowd turns at once, but the boy with the gun doesn't stop aiming at George, like I'd hoped.

"I've got you in my sights," I say. "Leave now and I'll let you go."

"I'll shoot him!" the boy says.

"I'll shoot *you*," I say. "We're with the government, but we aren't soldiers. We don't know where your people are. If you let him go, we'll all leave quietly. If you kill him, I guarantee there *will* be soldiers here soon to arrest you, and they won't be as forgiving as we are."

At that moment Amar emerges into the courtyard behind George, and someone in the crowd screeches,

"There are more of them!" And everyone scatters. The boy with the gun dives into the nearest aisle, leaving George, Amar, and me alone. Still, I keep my gun up by my face, in case they decide to come back.

Amar wraps his arms around George, and George thumps his back with a fist. Amar looks at me, his face over George's shoulder. "Still don't think genetic damage is to blame for any of these troubles?"

I walk past one of the lean-tos and see a little girl crouching just inside the door, her arms wrapped around her knees. She sees me through the crack in the layered tarps and whimpers a little. I wonder who taught these people to be so terrified of soldiers. I wonder what made a young boy desperate enough to aim a gun at one of them.

"No," I say. "I don't."

I have better people to blame.

+ + +

By the time we get back to the truck, Jack and Violet are setting up a surveillance camera that wasn't stolen by people in the fringe. Violet has a screen in her hands with a long list of numbers on it, and she reads them to Jack, who programs them into his screen.

"Where have you guys been?" he says.

"We were attacked," George says. "We have to leave, now."

"Luckily, that's the last set of coordinates," Violet says. "Let's get going."

We pile into the truck again. Amar draws the doors shut behind us, and I set my gun on the floor with the safety on, glad to be rid of it. I didn't think I would be aiming a dangerous weapon at someone today when I woke up. I didn't think I would witness those kinds of living conditions, either.

"It's the Abnegation in you," Amar says. "That makes you hate that place. I can tell."

"It's a lot of things in me."

"It's just something I noticed in Four, too. Abnegation produces deeply serious people. People who automatically see things like need," he says. "I've noticed that when people switch to Dauntless, it creates some of the same types. Erudite who switch to Dauntless tend to turn cruel and brutal. Candor who switch to Dauntless tend to become boisterous, fight-picking adrenaline junkies. And Abnegation who switch to Dauntless become . . . I don't know, soldiers, I guess. Revolutionaries.

"That's what he could be, if he trusted himself more," he adds. "If Four wasn't so plagued with self-doubt, he would be one hell of a leader, I think. I've always thought that."

"I think you're right," I say. "It's when he's a follower

that he gets himself into trouble. Like with Nita. Or Evelyn."

What about you? I ask myself. *You wanted to make him a follower too.*

No, I didn't, I tell myself, but I'm not sure if I believe it.

Amar nods.

Images from the fringe keep rising up inside me like hiccups. I imagine the child my mother was, crouched in one of those lean-tos, scrambling for weapons because they meant an ounce of safety, choking on smoke to keep warm in the winter. I don't know why she was so willing to abandon that place after she was rescued. She became absorbed into the compound, and then worked on its behalf for the rest of her life. Did she forget about where she came from?

She couldn't have. She spent her entire life trying to help the factionless. Maybe it wasn't a fulfillment of her duty as an Abnegation—maybe it came from a desire to help people like the ones she had left.

Suddenly I can't stand to think of her, or that place, or the things I saw there. I grab on to the first thought that comes to my mind, to distract myself.

"So you and Tobias were good friends?"

"Is anyone good friends with him?" Amar shakes his head. "I gave him his nickname, though. I watched him face his fears and I saw how troubled he was, and I figured he could use a new life, so I started calling him 'Four.' But no, I wouldn't say we were good friends. Not as good as I wanted to be."

Amar leans his head back against the wall and closes his eyes. A small smile curls his lips.

"Oh," I say. "Did you . . . *like* him?"

"Now why would you ask that?"

I shrug. "Just the way you talk about him."

"I don't *like* him anymore, if that's what you're really asking. But yes, at one time I did, and it was clear that he did not return that particular sentiment, so I backed off," Amar says. "I'd prefer it if you didn't say anything."

"To Tobias? Of course I won't."

"No, I mean, don't say anything to anyone. And I'm not talking about just the thing with Tobias."

He looks at the back of George's head, now visible above the considerably diminished pile of equipment.

I raise an eyebrow at him. I'm not surprised he and George were drawn to each other. They're both Divergent who had to fake their own deaths to survive. Both outsiders in an unfamiliar world.

"You have to understand," Amar says. "The Bureau is obsessed with procreation—with passing on genes. And George and I are both GPs, so any entanglement that can't produce a stronger genetic code . . . It's not encouraged, that's all."

"Ah." I nod. "You don't have to worry about me. I'm not obsessed with producing strong genes." I smile wryly.

"Thank you," he says.

For a few seconds we sit quietly, watching the ruins turn to a blur as the truck picks up speed.

"I think you're good for Four, you know," he says.

I stare at my hands, curled in my lap. I don't feel like explaining to him that we're on the verge of breaking up—I don't know him, and even if I did, I wouldn't want to talk about it. All I can manage to say is, "Oh?"

"Yeah. I can see what you bring out in him. You don't know this because you've never experienced it, but Four without you is a much different person. He's . . . obsessive, explosive, insecure . . ."

"Obsessive?"

"What else do you call someone who repeatedly goes through his own fear landscape?"

"I don't know . . . determined." I pause. "Brave."

"Yeah, sure. But also a little bit crazy, right? I mean, most Dauntless would rather leap into the chasm than keep going through their fear landscapes. There's bravery and then there's masochism, and the line got a little hazy with him."

"I'm familiar with the line," I say.

"I know." Amar grins. "Anyway, all I'm saying is, any time you mash two different people against each other, you'll get problems, but I can see that what you guys have is worthwhile, that's all."

I wrinkle my nose. "*Mash* people against each other, really?"

Amar presses his palms together and twists them back and forth, to illustrate. I laugh, but I can't ignore the achy feeling in my chest.

CHAPTER
THIRTY-FIVE

TOBIAS

I WALK TO the cluster of chairs closest to the windows in the control room and bring up the footage from different cameras throughout the city, one by one, searching for my parents. I find Evelyn first—she is in the lobby of Erudite headquarters, talking in a close huddle with Therese and a factionless man, her second and third in command now that I am gone. I turn up the volume on the microphone, but I still can't hear anything but muttering.

Through the windows along the back of the control room, I see the same empty night sky as the one above the city, interrupted only by small blue and red lights marking the runways for airplanes. It's strange to think we have that in common when everything else is so different here.

By now the people in the control room know that I was the one who disabled the security system the night before the attack, though I wasn't the one who slipped one of their night shift workers peace serum so that I could do it—that was Nita. But for the most part, they ignore me, as long as I stay away from their desks.

On another screen, I scroll through the footage again, looking for Marcus or Johanna, anything that can show me what's happening with the Allegiant. Every part of the city shows up on the screen, the bridge near the Merciless Mart and the Pire and the main thoroughfare of the Abnegation sector, the Hub and the Ferris wheel and the Amity fields, now worked by all the factions. But none of the cameras shows me anything.

"You've been coming here a lot," Cara says as she approaches. "Are you afraid of the rest of the compound? Or of something else?"

She's right, I have been coming to the control room a lot. It's just something to pass the time as I wait for my sentence from Tris, as I wait for our plan to strike the Bureau to come together, as I wait for something, *anything*.

"No," I say. "I'm just keeping an eye on my parents."

"The parents you hate?" She stands next to me, her arms folded. "Yes, I can see why you would want to spend every waking hour staring at people you want nothing to do with. It makes perfect sense."

"They're dangerous," I say. "More dangerous because no one else knows how dangerous they are but me."

"And what are you going to do from here, if they do something terrible? Send a smoke signal?"

I glare at her.

"Fine, fine." She puts up her hands in surrender. "I'm just trying to remind you that you aren't in their world anymore, you're in this one. That's all."

"Point taken."

I never thought of the Erudite as being particularly perceptive about relationships, or emotions, but Cara's discerning eyes see all kinds of things. My fear. My search for a distraction in my past. It's almost alarming.

I scroll past one of the camera angles and then pause, and scroll back. The scene is dark, because of the hour, but I see people alighting like a flock of birds around a building I don't recognize, their movements synchronized.

"They're doing it," Cara says, excited. "The Allegiant are actually attacking."

"Hey!" I shout to one of the women at the control room desks. The older one, who always gives me a nasty look when I show up, lifts her head. "Camera twenty-four! Hurry!"

She taps her screen, and everyone milling around the

Something about . . . no brain waves."

A weight settles on my shoulders. I knew, of course, that Uriah might never wake up. But the hope that kept the grief at bay is dwindling, slipping away with each word she speaks.

"They were going to take him off life support right away, but I pleaded with them." She wipes one of her eyes fiercely with the heel of her hand, catching a tear before it falls. "Finally the doctor said he would give me four days. So I can tell his family."

His family. Zeke is still in the city, and so is their Dauntless mother. It never occurred to me before that they don't know what happened to him, and we never bothered to tell them, because we were all so focused on—

"They're going to reset the city in forty-eight hours," I say suddenly, and I grab Tobias's arm. He looks stunned. "If we can't stop them, that means Zeke and his mother will *forget him*."

They'll forget him before they have a chance to say good-bye to him. It will be like he never existed.

"What?" Christina demands, her eyes wide. "My *family* is in there. They can't reset everyone! How could they do that?"

"Pretty easily, actually," Peter says. I had forgotten that he was there.

"What are you even doing here?" I demand.

"I went to see Uriah," he says. "Is there a law against it?"

"You didn't even care about him," I spit. "What right do you have—"

"Tris." Christina shakes her head. "Not now, okay?"

Tobias hesitates, his mouth open like there are words waiting on his tongue.

"We have to go in," he says. "Matthew said we could inoculate people against the memory serum, right? So we'll go in, inoculate Uriah's family just in case, and take them back to the compound to say good-bye to him. We have to do it tomorrow, though, or we'll be too late." He pauses. "And you can inoculate your family too, Christina. I should be the one who tells Zeke and Hana, anyway."

Christina nods. I squeeze her arm, in an attempt at reassurance.

"I'm going too," Peter says. "Unless you want me to tell David what you're planning."

We all pause to look at him. I don't know what Peter wants with a journey into the city, but it can't be good. At the same time, we can't afford for David to find out what we're doing, not now, when there's no time.

"Fine," Tobias says. "But if you cause any trouble, I reserve the right to knock you unconscious and lock you in an abandoned building somewhere."

Peter rolls his eyes.

"How do we get there?" Christina says. "It's not like they just let people borrow cars."

"I bet we could get Amar to take you," I say. "He told me today that he always volunteers for patrols. So he knows all the right people. And I'm sure he would agree to help Uriah and his family."

"I should go ask him now. And someone should probably sit with Uriah . . . make sure that doctor doesn't go back on his word. Christina, not Peter." Tobias rubs the back of his neck, pawing at the Dauntless tattoo like he wants to tear it from his body. "And then I should figure out how to tell Uriah's family that he got killed when I was supposed to be looking out for him."

"Tobias—" I say, but he holds up a hand to stop me.

He starts to move away. "They probably won't let me visit Nita anyway."

Sometimes it's hard to know how to take care of people. As I watch Peter and Tobias walk away—keeping their distance from each other—I think it's possible that Tobias needs someone to run after him, because people have been letting him walk away, letting him withdraw, his entire life. But he's right: He needs to do this for Zeke, and I need to talk to Nita.

"Come on," Christina says. "Visiting hours are almost over. I'm going back to sit with Uriah."

Before I go to Nita's room—identifiable by the security guard sitting by the door—I stop by Uriah's room with Christina. She sits in the chair next to him, which is creased with the contours of her legs.

It's been a long time since I've spoken to her like a friend, a long time since we laughed together. I was lost in the fog of the Bureau, in the promise of belonging.

I stand next to her and look at him. He doesn't really look injured anymore—there are some bruises, some cuts, but nothing serious enough to kill him. I tilt my head to see the snake tattoo wrapped around his ear. I know it's him, but he doesn't look much like Uriah without a wide smile on his face and his dark eyes bright, alert.

"He and I weren't really even that close," she says. "Just at the . . . the very end. Because he had lost someone who died, and so had I . . ."

"I know," I say. "You really helped him."

I drag a chair over to sit next to her. She clutches Uriah's hand, which stays limp on the sheets.

"Sometimes I just feel like I've lost all my friends," she says.

"You haven't lost Cara," I say. "Or Tobias. And Christina, you haven't lost me. You'll never lose me."

She turns to me, and somewhere in the haze of grief

we wrap our arms around each other, in the same desperate way we did when she told me she had forgiven me for killing Will. Our friendship has held up under an incredible weight, the weight of me shooting someone she loved, the weight of so many losses. Other bonds would have broken. For some reason, this one hasn't.

We stay clutched together for a long time, until the desperation fades.

"Thanks," she says. "You won't lose me, either."

"I'm pretty sure if I was going to, I would have already." I smile. "Listen, I have some things to catch you up on."

I tell her about our plan to stop the Bureau from resetting the experiments. As I speak, I think of the people she stands to lose—her father and mother, her sister—all those connections, forever altered or discarded, in the name of genetic purity.

"I'm sorry," I say when I finish. "I know you probably want to help us, but . . ."

"Don't be sorry." She stares at Uriah. "I'm still glad I'm going into the city." She nods a few times. "You'll stop them from resetting the experiment. I know you will."

I hope she's right.

+ + +

I only have ten minutes until visiting hours are over when I arrive at Nita's room. The guard looks up from his book and raises his eyebrow at me.

"Can I go in?" I say.

"Not really supposed to let people in there," he says.

"I'm the one who shot her," I say. "Does that count for anything?"

"Well." He shrugs. "As long as you promise not to shoot her again. And get out within ten minutes."

"It's a deal."

He has me take off my jacket to show that I'm not carrying any weapons, and then he lets me into the room. Nita jerks to attention—as much as she can, anyway. Half her body is encased in plaster, and one of her hands is cuffed to the bed, as if she could escape even if she wanted to. Her hair is messy, knotted, but of course, she's still pretty.

"What are you doing here?" she says.

I don't answer—I check the corners of the room for cameras, and there's one across from me, pointed at Nita's hospital bed.

"There aren't microphones," she says. "They don't really do that here."

"Good." I pull up a chair and sit beside her. "I'm here because I need important information from you."

"I already told them everything I felt like telling them." She glares at me. "I've got nothing more to say. Especially not to the person who shot me."

"If I hadn't shot you, I wouldn't be David's favorite person, and I wouldn't know all the things I know." I glance at the door, more from paranoia than an actual concern that someone is listening in. "We've got a new plan. Matthew and I. And Tobias. And it will require getting into the Weapons Lab."

"And you thought I could help you with that?" She shakes her head. "I couldn't get in the first time, remember?"

"I need to know what the security is like. Is David the only person who knows the pass code?"

"Not like . . . the only person ever," she says. "That would be stupid. His superiors know it, but he's the only person in the compound, yes."

"Okay, then what's the backup security measure? The one that is activated if you explode the doors?"

She presses her lips together so they almost disappear, and stares at the half-body cast covering her. "It's the death serum," she says. "In aerosol form, it's practically unstoppable. Even if you wear a clean suit or something, it works its way in eventually. It just takes a little more time that way. That's what the lab reports said."

"So they just automatically *kill* anyone who makes their way into that room without the pass code?" I say.

"It surprises you?"

"I guess not." I balance my elbows on my knees. "And there's no other way in except with David's code."

"Which, as you found out, he is completely unwilling to share," she says.

"There's no chance a GP could resist the death serum?" I say.

"No. Definitely not."

"Most GPs can't resist the truth serum, either," I say. "But I can."

"If you want to go flirt with death, be my guest." She leans back into the pillows. "I'm done with that now."

"One more question," I say. "Say I do want to flirt with death. Where do I get explosives to break through the doors?"

"Like I'm going to tell you that."

"I don't think you get it," I say. "If this plan succeeds, you won't be imprisoned for life anymore. You'll recover and you'll go free. So it's in your best interest to help me."

She stares at me like she is weighing and measuring me. Her wrist tugs against the handcuff, just enough that the metal carves a line into her skin.

"Reggie has the explosives," she says. "He can teach you how to use them, but he's no good in action, so for God's sake, don't bring him along unless you feel like babysitting."

"Noted," I say.

"Tell him it will require twice as much firepower to get through those doors than any others. They're extremely sturdy."

I nod. My watch beeps on the hour, signaling that my time is up. I stand and push my chair back to the corner where I found it.

"Thank you for the help," I say.

"What is the plan?" she says. "If you don't mind telling me."

I pause, hesitating over the words.

"Well," I say eventually. "Let's just say it will erase the phrase 'genetically damaged' from everyone's vocabulary."

The guard opens the door, probably to yell at me for overstaying my welcome, but I'm already making my way out. I look over my shoulder just once before going, and I see that Nita is wearing a small smile.

CHAPTER
FORTY

AMAR AGREES TO help us get into the city without requiring much persuasion, eager for an adventure, as I knew he would be. We agree to meet that evening for dinner to talk through the plan with Christina, Peter, and George, who will help us get a vehicle.

After I talk to Amar, I walk to the dormitory and lay with a pillow over my head for a long time, cycling through a script of what I will say to Zeke when I see him. *I'm sorry, I was doing what I thought I had to do, and everyone else was looking after Uriah, and I didn't think . . .*

People come into the room and leave it, the heat switches on and pushes through the vents and then turns off again, and all the while I am thinking through that script, concocting excuses and then discarding them, choosing the right tone, the right gestures. Finally I grow frustrated and take the pillow from my face and fling it against the opposite wall. Cara, who is just smoothing a clean shirt down over her hips, jumps back.

"I thought you were asleep," she says.

"Sorry."

She touches her hair, ensuring that each strand is secure. She is so careful in her movements, so precise—it reminds me of the Amity musicians plucking at banjo strings.

"I have a question." I sit up. "It's kind of personal."

"Okay." She sits across from me, on Tris's bed. "Ask it."

"How were you able to forgive Tris, after what she did to your brother?" I say. "Assuming you have, that is."

"Hmm." Cara hugs her arms close to her body. "Sometimes I think I have forgiven her. Sometimes I'm not certain I have. I don't know how—that's like asking how you continue on with your life after someone dies. You just do it, and the next day you do it again."

"Is there . . . any way she could have made it easier for you? Or any way she did?"

"Why are you asking this?" She sets her hand on my knee. "Is it because of Uriah?"

"Yes," I say firmly, and I shift my leg a little so her hand falls away. I don't need to be patted or consoled, like a child. I don't need her raised eyebrows, her soft voice, to coax an emotion from me that I would prefer to contain.

"Okay." She straightens, and when she speaks again, she sounds casual, the way she usually does. "I think the most crucial thing she did—admittedly without meaning to—was confess. There is a difference between admitting and confessing. Admitting involves softening, making excuses for things that cannot be excused; confessing just names the crime at its full severity. That was something I needed."

I nod.

"And after you've confessed to Zeke," she says, "I think it would help if you leave him alone for as long as he wants to be left alone. That's all you can do."

I nod again.

"But, Four," she adds, "you didn't kill Uriah. You didn't set off the bomb that injured him. You didn't make the plan that led to that explosion."

"But I did participate in the plan."

"Oh, shut up, would you?" She says it gently, smiling at me. "It happened. It was awful. You aren't perfect. That's all there is. Don't confuse your grief with guilt."

We stay in the silence and the loneliness of the otherwise empty dormitory for a few more minutes, and I try to let her words work themselves into me.

I eat dinner with Amar, George, Christina, and Peter in the cafeteria, between the beverage counter and a row of trash cans. The bowl of soup before me went cold before I could eat all of it, and there are still crackers swimming in the broth.

Amar tells us where and when to meet, then we go to the hallway near the kitchens so we won't be seen, and he takes out a small black box with syringes inside it. He gives one to Christina, Peter, and me, along with an individually packaged antibacterial wipe, something I suspect only Amar will bother with.

"What's this?" Christina says. "I'm not going to inject it into my body unless I know what it is."

"Fine." Amar folds his hands. "There's a chance that we will still be in the city when a memory serum virus is deployed. You'll need to inoculate yourself against it unless you want to forget everything you now remember. It's the same thing you'll be injecting into your family's arms, so don't worry about it."

Christina turns her arm over and slaps the inside of her elbow until a vein stands at attention. Out of habit, I stick the needle into the side of my neck, the same way I did every time I went through my fear landscape—which was several times a week, at one point. Amar does the same thing.

I notice, however, that Peter only pretends to inject himself—when he presses the plunger down, the fluid runs down his throat, and he wipes it casually with a sleeve.

I wonder what it feels like to volunteer to forget everything.

+ + +

After dinner Christina walks up to me and says, "We need to talk."

We walk down the long flight of stairs that leads to the underground GD space, our knees bouncing in unison with each step, and down the multicolored hallway. At the end, Christina crosses her arms, purple light playing over her nose and mouth.

"Amar doesn't know we're going to try to stop the reset?" she says.

"No," I say. "He's loyal to the Bureau. I don't want to involve him."

"You know, the city is still on the verge of revolution," she says, and the light turns blue. "The Bureau's whole reason for resetting our friends and families is to stop them from killing each other. If we stop the reset, the Allegiant will attack Evelyn, Evelyn will turn the death serum loose, and a lot of people will die. I may still be mad at you, but I don't think you want that many people in the city to die. Your parents in particular."

I sigh. "Honestly? I don't really care about them."

"You can't be serious," she says, scowling. "They're your *parents*."

"I can be, actually," I say. "I want to tell Zeke and his mother what I did to Uriah. Apart from that, I really don't care what happens to Evelyn and Marcus."

"You may not care about your permanently messed-up family, but you should care about everyone else!" she says. She takes my arm in one strong hand and jerks me so that I look at her. "Four, my little sister is in there. If Evelyn and the Allegiant smack into each other, she could get hurt, and I won't be there to protect her."

I saw Christina with her family on Visiting Day, when she was still just a loudmouthed Candor transfer to me. I watched her mother fix the collar of Christina's shirt with a proud smile. If the memory serum virus is deployed, that memory will be erased from her mother's mind. If it's not, her family will be caught in the middle of another citywide battle for control.

I say, "So what are you suggesting we do?"

She releases me. "There has to be a way to prevent a huge blowup that doesn't involve forcibly erasing everyone's memories."

"Maybe," I concede. I hadn't thought about it because it didn't seem necessary. But it is necessary, of course it's necessary. "Did you have an idea for how to stop it?"

"It's basically one of your parents against the other one," Christina says. "Isn't there something you can say to them that will stop them from trying to kill each other?"

"Something I can *say* to them?" I say. "Are you kidding? They don't listen to anyone. They don't do anything that doesn't directly benefit them."

"So there's nothing you can do. You're just going to let the city rip itself to shreds."

I stare at my shoes, bathed in green light, mulling it over. If I had different parents—if I had reasonable parents, less driven by pain and anger and the desire for revenge—it might work. They might be compelled to listen to their son. Unfortunately, I do not have different parents.

But I could. I could if I wanted them. Just a slip of the memory serum in their morning coffee or their evening water, and they would be new people, clean slates, unblemished by history. They would have to be taught that they even had a son to begin with; they would need to learn my name again.

It's the same technique we're using to heal the compound. I could use it to heal them.

I look up at Christina.

"Get me some memory serum," I say. "While you, Amar, and Peter are looking for your family and Uriah's family, I'll take care of it. I probably won't have enough time to get to both of my parents, but one of them will do."

"How will you get away from the rest of us?"

"I need . . . I don't know, we need to add a complication. Something that requires one of us leaving the pack."

"What about flat tires?" Christina says. "We're going at night, right? So I can tell Amar to stop so I can go to the bathroom or something, slash the tires, and then we'll have to split up, so you can find another truck."

I consider this for a moment. I could tell Amar what's really going on, but that would require undoing the dense knot of propaganda and lies the Bureau has tied in his mind. Assuming I could even do it, we don't have time for that.

But we do have time for a well-told lie. Amar knows that my father taught me how to start a car with just the wires when I was younger. He wouldn't question me volunteering to find us another vehicle.

"That will work," I say.

"Good." She tilts her head. "So you're really going to erase one of your parents' memories?"

"What do you do when your parents are evil?" I say.

"Get a new parent. If one of them doesn't have all the baggage they currently have, maybe the two of them can negotiate a peace agreement or something."

She frowns at me for a few seconds like she wants to say something, but eventually, she just nods.

CHAPTER
FORTY-ONE

TRIS

THE SMELL OF bleach tingles in my nose. I stand next to a mop in a storage room in the basement; I stand in the wake of what I just told everyone, which is that whoever breaks into the Weapons Lab will be going on a suicide mission. The death serum is unstoppable.

"The question is," Matthew says, "is this something we're willing to sacrifice a life for."

This is the room where Matthew, Caleb, and Cara were developing the new serum, before the plan changed. Vials and beakers and scribbled-on notebooks are scattered across the lab table in front of Matthew. The string he wears tied around his neck is in his mouth now, and he chews it absentmindedly.

Tobias leans against the door, his arms crossed. I

remember him standing that way during initiation, as he watched us fight each other, so tall and so strong I never dreamed he would give me more than a cursory glance.

"It's not just about revenge," I say. "It's not about what they did to the Abnegation. It's about stopping them before they do something equally bad to the people in all the experiments—about taking away their power to control thousands of lives."

"It is worth it," Cara says. "One death, to save thousands of people from a terrible fate? And cut the compound's power off at the knees, so to speak? Is it even a question?"

I know what she is doing—weighing a single life against so many lifetimes and memories, drawing an obvious conclusion from the scales. That is the way an Erudite mind works, and the way an Abnegation mind works, but I am not sure if they are the minds we need right now. One life against thousands of memories, of course the answer is easy, but does it have to be one of our lives? Do we have to be the ones who act?

But because I know what my answer will be to that question, my thoughts turn to another question. If it has to be one of us, who should it be?

My eyes shift from Matthew and Cara, standing behind the table, to Tobias, to Christina, her arm slung over a broom handle, and land on Caleb.

Him.

A second later I feel sick with myself.

"Oh, just come out with it," Caleb says, lifting his eyes to mine. "You want me to do it. You all do."

"No one said that," Matthew says, spitting out the string necklace.

"Everyone's staring at me," Caleb says. "Don't think I don't know it. I'm the one who chose the wrong side, who worked with Jeanine Matthews; I'm the one none of you care about, so I should be the one to die."

"Why do you think Tobias offered to get you out of the city before they executed you?" My voice comes out cold, quiet. The odor of bleach plays over my nose. "Because I don't care whether you live or die? Because I don't care about you at all?"

He should be the one to die, part of me thinks.

I don't want to lose him, another part argues.

I don't know which part to trust, which part to believe.

"You think I don't know hatred when I see it?" Caleb shakes his head. "I see it every time you look at me. On the rare occasions when you do look at me."

His eyes are glossy with tears. It's the first time since my near execution that I've seen him remorseful instead of defensive or full of excuses. It might also be the first time since then that I've seen him as my brother instead of the coward who sold me out to Jeanine Matthews. Suddenly I have trouble swallowing.

"If I do this . . ." he says.

I shake my head no, but he holds up a hand.

"Stop," he says. "Beatrice, if I do this . . . will you be able to forgive me?"

To me, when someone wrongs you, you both share the burden of that wrongdoing—the pain of it weighs on both of you. Forgiveness, then, means choosing to bear the full weight all by yourself. Caleb's betrayal is something we both carry, and since he did it, all I've wanted is for him to take its weight away from me. I am not sure that I'm capable of shouldering it all myself—not sure that I am strong enough, or good enough.

But I see him steeling himself against this fate, and I know that I *have* to be strong enough, and good enough, if he is going to sacrifice himself for us all.

I nod. "Yes," I choke out. "But that's not a good reason to do this."

"I have plenty of reasons," Caleb says. "I'll do it. Of course I will."

+ + +

I am not sure what just happened.

Matthew and Caleb stay behind to fit Caleb for the clean suit—the suit that will keep him alive in the Weapons Lab long enough to set off the memory serum virus. I wait until the others leave before leaving myself. I want to walk back to the dormitory with only my thoughts as company.

A few weeks ago, I would have volunteered to go on the suicide mission myself—and I did. I volunteered to go to Erudite headquarters, knowing that death waited for me there. But it wasn't because I was selfless, or because I was brave. It was because I was guilty and a part of me wanted to lose everything; a grieving, ailing part of me wanted to die. Is that what's motivating Caleb now? Should I really allow him to die so that he feels like his debt to me is repaid?

I walk the hallway with its rainbow of lights and go up the stairs. I can't even think of an alternative—would I be any more willing to lose Christina, or Cara, or Matthew? No. The truth is that I would be less willing to lose them, because they have been good friends to me and Caleb has not, not for a long time. Even before he betrayed me, he left me for the Erudite and didn't look back. I was the one who went to visit *him* during my initiation, and he spent the whole time wondering why I was there.

And I don't want to die anymore. I am up to the challenge of bearing the guilt and the grief, up to facing the difficulties that life has put in my path. Some days are harder than others, but I am ready to live each one of them. I can't sacrifice myself, this time.

In the most honest parts of me, I am able to admit that it was a relief to hear Caleb volunteer.

Suddenly I can't think about it anymore. I reach the hotel entrance and walk to the dormitory, hoping that I can just collapse into my bed and sleep, but Tobias is waiting in the hallway for me.

"You okay?" he says.

"Yes," I say. "But I shouldn't be." I touch a hand, briefly, to my forehead. "I feel like I've already been mourning him. Like he died the second I saw him in Erudite headquarters while I was there. You know?"

I confessed to Tobias, soon after that, that I had lost my entire family. And he assured me that he was my family now.

That is how it feels. Like everything between us is twisted together, friendship and love and family, so I can't tell the difference between any of them.

"The Abnegation have teachings about this, you know," he says. "About when to let others sacrifice themselves for you, even if it's selfish. They say that if the sacrifice is the ultimate way for that person to show you that they love you, you should let them do it." He leans one shoulder into the wall. "That, in that situation, it's the greatest gift you can give them. Just as it was when both of your parents died for you."

"I'm not sure it's love that's motivating him, though." I close my eyes. "It seems more like guilt."

"Maybe," Tobias admits. "But why would he feel guilty for betraying you if he didn't love you?"

I nod. I know that Caleb loves me, and always has, even when he was hurting me. I know that I love him, too. But this feels wrong anyway.

Still, I am able to be momentarily placated, knowing that this is something my parents might have understood, if they were here right now.

"This may be a bad time," he says, "but there's something I want to say to you."

I tense immediately, afraid that he's going to name some crime of mine that went unacknowledged, or a confession that's eating away at him, or something equally difficult. His expression is unreadable.

"I just want to thank you," he says, his voice low. "A group of scientists told you that my genes were damaged, that there was something wrong with me—they showed you test results that proved it. And even I started to believe it."

He touches my face, his thumb skimming my cheekbone, and his eyes are on mine, intense and insistent.

"You never believed it," he says. "Not for a second. You always insisted that I was . . . I don't know, whole."

I hesitate, my hand on the vial in my pocket. I look at her, and I can see the way time has worn through her like an old piece of cloth, the fibers exposed and fraying. And I can see the woman I knew as a child, too, the mouth that stretched into a smile, the eyes that sparkled with joy. But the longer I look at her, the more convinced I am that that happy woman never existed. That woman is just a pale version of my real mother, viewed through the self-centered eyes of a child.

I sit down across from her at the table and put the vial of memory serum between us.

"I came to make you drink this," I say.

She looks at the vial, and I think I see tears in her eyes, but it could just be the light.

"I thought it was the only way to prevent total destruction," I say. "I know that Marcus and Johanna and their people are going to attack, and I know that you will do whatever it takes to stop them, including using that death serum you possess to its best advantage." I tilt my head. "Am I wrong?"

"No," she says. "The factions are evil. They cannot be restored. I would sooner see us all destroyed."

Her hand squeezes the edge of the table, the knuckles pale.

"The reason the factions were evil is because there

was no way out of them," I say. "They gave us the illusion of choice without actually giving us a choice. That's the same thing you're doing here, by abolishing them. You're saying, go make choices. But make sure they aren't factions or I'll grind you to bits!"

"If you thought that, why didn't you tell me?" she says, her voice louder and her eyes avoiding mine, avoiding me. "Tell me, instead of *betraying* me?"

"Because I'm afraid of you!" The words burst out, and I regret them but I'm also glad they're there, glad that before I ask her to give up her identity, I can at least be honest with her. "You . . . you remind me of *him*!"

"Don't you dare." She clenches her hands into fists and almost spits at me, "Don't you *dare*."

"I don't care if you don't want to hear it," I say, coming to my feet. "He was a tyrant in our house and now you're a tyrant in this city, and you can't even see that it's the same!"

"So that's why you brought this," she says, and she wraps her hand around the vial, holding it up to look at it. "Because you think this is the only way to mend things."

"I . . ." I am about to say that it's the easiest way, the best way, maybe the only way that I can trust her.

If I erase her memories, I can create for myself a new mother, but.

But she is more than my mother. She is a person in her

own right, and she does not belong to me.

I do not get to choose what she becomes just because I can't deal with who she is.

"No," I say. "No, I came to give you a choice."

I feel suddenly terrified, my hands numb, my heart beating fast—

"I thought about going to see Marcus tonight, but I didn't." I swallow hard. "I came to see you instead because . . . because I think there's a hope of reconciliation between us. Not now, not soon, but someday. And with him there's no hope, there's no reconciliation possible."

She stares at me, her eyes fierce but welling up with tears.

"It's not fair for me to give you this choice," I say. "But I have to. You can lead the factionless, you can fight the Allegiant, but you'll have to do it without me, forever. Or you can let this crusade go, and . . . and you'll have your son back."

It's a feeble offer and I know it, which is why I'm afraid—afraid that she will refuse to choose, that she will choose power over me, that she will call me a ridiculous child, which is what I am. I am a child. I am two feet tall and asking her how much she loves me.

Evelyn's eyes, dark as wet earth, search mine for a long time.

Then she reaches across the table and pulls me fiercely

into her arms, which form a wire cage around me, surprisingly strong.

"Let them have the city and everything in it," she says into my hair.

I can't move, can't speak. She chose me. She chose me.

CHAPTER
FORTY-NINE

TRIS

THE DEATH SERUM smells like smoke and spice, and my lungs reject it with the first breath I take. I cough and splutter, and I am swallowed by darkness.

I crumple to my knees. My body feels like someone has replaced my blood with molasses, and my bones with lead. An invisible thread tugs me toward sleep, but I want to be awake. It is important that I want to be awake. I imagine that wanting, that desire, burning in my chest like a flame.

The thread tugs harder, and I stoke the flame with names. Tobias. Caleb. Christina. Matthew. Cara. Zeke. Uriah.

But I can't bear up under the serum's weight. My body

falls to the side, and my wounded arm presses to the cold ground. I am drifting. . . .

It would be nice to float away, a voice in my head says. *To see where I will go . . .*

But the fire, the fire.

The desire to live.

I am not done yet, I am not.

I feel like I am digging through my own mind. It is difficult to remember why I came here and why I care about unburdening myself from this beautiful weight. But then my scratching hands find it, the memory of my mother's face, and the strange angles of her limbs on the pavement, and the blood seeping from my father's body.

But they are dead, the voice says. *You could join them.*

They died for me, I answer. And now I have something to do, in return. I have to stop other people from losing everything. I have to save the city and the people my mother and father loved.

If I go to join my parents, I want to carry with me a good *reason*, not this—this senseless collapsing at the threshold.

The fire, the fire. It rages within, a campfire and then an inferno, and my body is its fuel. I feel it racing through me, eating away at the weight. There is nothing that can kill me now; I am powerful and invincible and eternal.

I feel the serum clinging to my skin like oil, but the darkness recedes. I slap a heavy hand over the floor and push myself up.

Bent at the waist, I shove my shoulder into the double doors, and they squeak across the floor as their seal breaks. I breathe clean air and stand up straighter. I am there, I am *there*.

But I am not alone.

"Don't move," David says, raising his gun. "Hello, Tris."

CHAPTER FIFTY

TRIS

"HOW DID YOU inoculate yourself against the death serum?" he asks me. He's still sitting in his wheelchair, but you don't need to be able to walk to fire a gun.

I blink at him, still dazed.

"I didn't," I say.

"Don't be stupid," David says. "You can't survive the death serum without an inoculation, and I'm the only person in the compound who possesses that substance."

I just stare at him, not sure what to say. I didn't inoculate myself. The fact that I'm still standing upright is impossible. There's nothing more to add.

"I suppose it no longer matters," he says. "We're here now."

"What are you doing here?" I mumble. My lips feel awkwardly large, hard to talk around. I still feel that oily heaviness on my skin, like death is clinging to me even though I have defeated it.

I am dimly aware that I left my own gun in the hallway behind me, sure I wouldn't need it if I made it this far.

"I knew something was going on," David says. "You've been running around with genetically damaged people all week, Tris, did you think I wouldn't notice?" He shakes his head. "And then your friend Cara was caught trying to manipulate the lights, but she very wisely knocked herself out before she could tell us anything. So I came here, just in case. I'm sad to say I'm not surprised to see you."

"You came here alone?" I say. "Not very smart, are you?"

His bright eyes squint a little. "Well, you see, I have death serum resistance and a weapon, and you have no way to fight me. There's no way you can steal four virus devices while I have you at gunpoint. I'm afraid you've come all this way for no reason, and it will be at the expense of your life. The death serum may not have killed you, but I am going to. I'm sure you understand—officially we don't allow capital punishment, but I can't have you surviving this."

He thinks I'm here to steal the weapons that will reset the experiments, not deploy one of them. Of course he does.

I try to guard my expression, though I'm sure it's still slack. I sweep my eyes across the room, searching for the device that will release the memory serum virus. I was there when Matthew described it to Caleb in painstaking detail earlier: a black box with a silver keypad, marked with a strip of blue tape with a model number written on it. It is one of the only items on the counter along the left wall, just a few feet away from me. But I can't move, or else he'll kill me.

I'll have to wait for the right moment, and do it fast.

"I know what you did," I say. I start to back up, hoping that the accusation will distract him. "I know you designed the attack simulation. I know you're responsible for my parents' deaths—for my *mother's* death. I know."

"I am not responsible for her death!" David says, the words bursting from him, too loud and too sudden. "I *told* her what was coming just before the attack began, so she had enough time to escort her loved ones to a safe house. If she had stayed put, she would have lived. But she was a foolish woman who didn't understand making sacrifices for the greater good, and it *killed* her!"

I frown at him. There's something about his reaction—about the glassiness of his eyes—something that he mumbled when Nita shot him with the fear serum—something about *her*.

"Did you love her?" I say. "All those years she was sending you correspondence . . . the reason you never wanted her to stay there . . . the reason you told her you couldn't read her updates anymore, after she married my father . . ."

David sits still, like a statue, like a man of stone.

"I did," he says. "But that time is past."

That must be why he welcomed me into his circle of trust, why he gave me so many opportunities. Because I am a piece of her, wearing her hair and speaking with her voice. Because he has spent his life grasping at her and coming up with nothing.

I hear footsteps in the hallway outside. The soldiers are coming. Good—I need them to. I need them to be exposed to the airborne serum, to pass it on to the rest of the compound. I hope they wait until the air is clear of death serum.

"My mother wasn't a fool," I say. "She just understood something you didn't. That it's not sacrifice if it's someone *else's* life you're giving away, it's just evil."

I back up another step and say, "She taught me all about real sacrifice. That it should be done from love, not misplaced disgust for another person's genetics. That it should be done from necessity, not without exhausting all other options. That it should be done for people who need your strength because they don't have enough of their own. That's why I need to stop you from 'sacrificing' all those people and their memories. Why I need to rid the world of you once and for all."

I shake my head.

"I didn't come here to steal anything, David."

I twist and lunge toward the device. The gun goes off and pain races through my body. I don't even know where the bullet hit me.

I can still hear Caleb repeating the code for Matthew. With a quaking hand I type in the numbers on the keypad.

The gun goes off again.

More pain, and black edges on my vision, but I hear Caleb's voice speaking again. *The green button.*

So much pain.

But how, when my body feels so numb?

I start to fall, and slam my hand into the keypad on my way down. A light turns on behind the green button.

I hear a beep, and a churning sound.

I slide to the floor. I feel something warm on my neck, and under my cheek. Red. Blood is a strange color. Dark.

From the corner of my eye, I see David slumped over in his chair.

And my *mother* walking out from behind him.

She is dressed in the same clothes she wore the last

time I saw her, Abnegation gray, stained with her blood, with bare arms to show her tattoo. There are still bullet holes in her shirt; through them I can see her wounded skin, red but no longer bleeding, like she's frozen in time. Her dull blond hair is tied back in a knot, but a few loose strands frame her face in gold.

I know she can't be alive, but I don't know if I'm seeing her now because I'm delirious from the blood loss or if the death serum has addled my thoughts or if she is here in some other way.

She kneels next to me and touches a cool hand to my cheek.

"Hello, Beatrice," she says, and she smiles.

"Am I done yet?" I say, and I'm not sure if I actually say it or if I just think it and she hears it.

"Yes," she says, her eyes bright with tears. "My dear child, you've done so well."

"What about the others?" I choke on a sob as the image of Tobias comes into my mind, of how dark and how still his eyes were, how strong and warm his hand was, when we first stood face-to-face. "Tobias, Caleb, my friends?"

"They'll care for each other," she says. "That's what people do."

I smile and close my eyes.

I feel a thread tugging me again, but this time I know that it isn't some sinister force dragging me toward death.

This time I know it's my mother's hand, drawing me into her arms.

And I go gladly into her embrace.

+ + +

Can I be forgiven for all I've done to get here?

I want to be.

I can.

I believe it.

CHAPTER FIFTY-ONE

TOBIAS

EVELYN BRUSHES THE tears from her eyes with her thumb. We stand by the windows, shoulder to shoulder, watching the snow swirl past. Some of the flakes gather on the windowsill outside, piling at the corners.

The feeling has returned to my hands. As I stare out at the world, dusted in white, I feel like everything has begun again, and it will be better this time.

"I think I can get in touch with Marcus over the radio to negotiate a peace agreement," Evelyn says. "He'll be listening in; he'd be stupid not to."

"Before you do that, I made a promise I have to keep," I say. I touch Evelyn's shoulder. I expected to see strain at the edges of her smile, but I don't.

I feel a twinge of guilt. I didn't come here to ask her to lay down arms for me, to trade in everything she's worked for just to get me back. But then again, I didn't come here to give her any choice at all. I guess Tris was right—when you have to choose between two bad options, you pick the one that saves the people you love. I wouldn't have been saving Evelyn by giving her that serum. I would have been destroying her.

Peter sits with his back to the wall in the hallway. He looks up at me when I lean over him, his dark hair stuck to his forehead from the melted snow.

"Did you reset her?" he says.

"No," I say.

"Didn't think you would have the nerve."

"It's not about nerve. You know what? Whatever." I shake my head and hold up the vial of memory serum. "Are you still set on this?"

He nods.

"You could just do the work, you know," I say. "You could make better decisions, make a better life."

"Yeah, I could," he says. "But I won't. We both know that."

I do know that. I know that change is difficult, and comes slowly, and that it is the work of many days strung together in a long line until the origin of them is forgotten. He is afraid that he will not be able to put in that work, that he will squander those days, and that they will leave him worse off than he is now. And I understand that feeling—I understand being afraid of yourself.

So I have him sit on one of the couches, and I ask him what he wants me to tell him about himself, after his memories disappear like smoke. He just shakes his head. Nothing. He wants to retain nothing.

Peter takes the vial with a shaking hand and twists off the cap. The liquid trembles inside it, almost spilling over the lip. He holds it under his nose to smell it.

"How much should I drink?" he says, and I think I hear his teeth chattering.

"I don't think it makes a difference," I say.

"Okay. Well . . . here goes." He lifts the vial up to the light like he is toasting me.

When he touches it to his mouth, I say, "Be brave."

Then he swallows.

And I watch Peter disappear.

+ + +

The air outside tastes like ice.

"Hey! Peter!" I shout, my breaths turning to vapor.

Peter stands by the doorway to Erudite headquarters, looking clueless. At the sound of his name—which I have told him at least ten times since he drank the serum—he raises his eyebrows, pointing to his chest. Matthew told us people would be disoriented for a while after drinking the memory serum, but I didn't think "disoriented" meant "stupid" until now.

I sigh. "Yes, that's you! For the eleventh time! Come on, let's go."

I thought that when I looked at him after he drank the serum, I would still see the initiate who shoved a butter knife into Edward's eye, and the boy who tried to kill my girlfriend, and all the other things he has done, stretching backward for as long as I've known him. But it's easier than I thought to see that he has no idea who he is anymore. His eyes still have that wide, innocent look, but this time, I believe it.

Evelyn and I walk side by side, with Peter trotting behind us. The snow has stopped falling now, but enough has collected on the ground that it squeaks under my shoes.

We walk to Millennium Park, where the mammoth bean sculpture reflects the moonlight, and then down a set of stairs. As we descend, Evelyn wraps her hand around my elbow to keep her balance, and we exchange a look. I wonder if she is as nervous as I am to face my father again. I wonder if she is nervous every time.

At the bottom of the steps is a pavilion with two glass blocks, each one at least three times as tall as I am, at either end. This is where we told Marcus and Johanna we would meet them—both parties armed, to be realistic but even.

They are already there. Johanna isn't holding a gun, but Marcus is, and he has it trained on Evelyn. I point the gun Evelyn gave me at him, just to be safe. I notice the planes of his skull, showing through his shaved hair, and the jagged path his crooked nose carves down his face.

"Tobias!" Johanna says. She wears a coat in Amity red, dusted with snowflakes. "What are you doing here?"

"Trying to keep you all from killing each other," I say. "I'm surprised you're carrying a gun."

I nod to the bulge in her coat pocket, the unmistakable contours of a weapon.

"Sometimes you have to take difficult measures to ensure peace," Johanna says. "I believe you agree with that, as a principle."

"We're not here to chat," Marcus says, looking at Evelyn. "You said you wanted to talk about a treaty."

The past few weeks have taken something from him. I can see it in the turned-down corners of his mouth, in the purple skin under his eyes. I see my own eyes set into his skull, and I think of my reflection in the fear landscape, how terrified I was, watching his skin spread over mine like a rash. I am still nervous that I will become him, even now, standing at odds with him with my mother at my side, like I always dreamed I would when I was a child.

But I don't think that I'm still afraid.

"Yes," Evelyn says. "I have some terms for us both to agree to. I think you will find them fair. If you agree to them, I will step down and surrender whatever weapons I have that my people are not using for personal protection. I will leave the city and not return."

Marcus laughs. I'm not sure if it's a mocking laugh or a disbelieving one. He's equally capable of either sentiment, an arrogant and deeply suspicious man.

"Let her finish," Johanna says quietly, tucking her hands into her sleeves.

"In return," Evelyn says, "you will not attack or try to seize control of the city. You will allow those people who wish to leave and seek a new life elsewhere to do so. You will allow those who choose to stay to *vote* on new leaders and a new social system. And most importantly, *you*, Marcus, will not be eligible to lead them."

It is the only purely selfish term of the peace agreement. She told me she couldn't stand the thought of Marcus duping more people into following him, and I didn't argue with her.

Johanna raises her eyebrows. I notice that she has pulled her hair back on both sides, to reveal the scar in its entirety. She looks better that way—stronger, when she is not hiding behind a curtain of hair, hiding who she is.

"No deal," Marcus says. "I am the leader of these people."

"Marcus," Johanna says.

He ignores her. "*You* don't get to decide whether I lead them or not because you have a grudge against me, Evelyn!"

"Excuse me," Johanna says loudly. "Marcus, what she is offering is too good to be true—we get everything we want without all the violence! How can you possibly say no?"

"Because I am the rightful leader of these people!" Marcus says. "I am the leader of the Allegiant! I—"

"No, you are not," Johanna says calmly. "*I* am the leader of the Allegiant. And you are going to agree to this treaty, or I am going to tell them that you had a chance to end this conflict without bloodshed if you sacrificed your pride, and you said no."

Marcus's passive mask is gone, revealing the malicious face beneath it. But even he can't argue with Johanna, whose perfect calm and perfect threat have mastered him. He shakes his head but doesn't argue again.

"I agree to your terms," Johanna says, and she holds out

her hand, her footsteps squeaking in the snow.

Evelyn removes her glove fingertip by fingertip, reaches across the gap, and shakes.

"In the morning we should gather everyone together and tell them the new plan," Johanna says. "Can you guarantee a safe gathering?"

"I'll do my best," Evelyn says.

I check my watch. An hour has passed since Amar and Christina separated from us near the Hancock building, which means he probably knows that the serum virus didn't work. Or maybe he doesn't. Either way, I have to do what I came here to do—I have to find Zeke and his mother and tell them what happened to Uriah.

"I should go," I say to Evelyn. "I have something else to take care of. But I'll pick you up from the city limits tomorrow afternoon?"

"That sounds good," Evelyn says, and she rubs my arm briskly with a gloved hand, like she used to when I came in from the cold as a child.

"You won't be back, I assume?" Johanna says to me. "You've found a life for yourself on the outside?"

"I have," I say. "Good luck in here. The people outside—they're going to try to shut the city down. You should be ready for them."

Johanna smiles. "I'm sure we can negotiate with them."

She offers me her hand, and I shake it. I feel Marcus's eyes on me like an oppressive weight threatening to crush me. I force myself to look at him.

"Good-bye," I say to him, and I mean it.

+ + +

Hana, Zeke's mother, has small feet that don't touch the ground when she sits in the easy chair in their living room. She is wearing a ragged black bathrobe and slippers, but the air she has, with her hands folded in her lap and her eyebrows raised, is so dignified that I feel like I am standing in front of a world leader. I glance at Zeke, who is rubbing his face with his fists to wake up.

Amar and Christina found them, not among the other revolutionaries near the Hancock building, but in their family apartment in the Pire, above Dauntless headquarters. I only found them because Christina thought to leave Peter and me a note with their location on the useless truck. Peter is waiting in the new van Evelyn found for us to drive to the Bureau.

"I'm sorry," I say. "I don't know where to start."

"You might begin with the worst," Hana says. "Like what exactly happened to my son."

"He was seriously injured during an attack," I say. "There was an explosion, and he was very close to it."

"Oh God," Zeke says, and he rocks back and forth like

his body wants to be a child again, soothed by motion as a child is.

But Hana just bends her head, hiding her face from me.

Their living room smells like garlic and onion, maybe remnants from that night's dinner. I lean my shoulder into the white wall by the doorway. Hanging crookedly next to me is a picture of the family—Zeke as a toddler, Uriah as a baby, balancing on his mother's lap. Their father's face is pierced in several places, nose and ear and lip, but his wide, bright smile and dark complexion are more familiar to me, because he passed them both to his sons.

"He has been in a coma since then," I say. "And . . ."

"And he isn't going to wake up," Hana says, her voice strained. "That is what you came to tell us, right?"

"Yes," I say. "I came to collect you so that you can make a decision on his behalf."

"A decision?" Zeke says. "You mean, to *unplug* him or not?"

"Zeke," Hana says, and she shakes her head. He sinks back into the couch. The cushions seem to wrap around him.

"Of course we don't want to keep him alive that way," Hana says. "He would want to move on. But we would like to go see him."

I nod. "Of course. But there's something else I should

say. The attack . . . it was a kind of uprising that involved some of the people from the place where we were staying. And I participated in it."

I stare at the crack in the floorboards right in front of me, at the dust that has gathered there over time, and wait for a reaction, any reaction. What greets me is only silence.

"I didn't do what you asked me," I say to Zeke. "I didn't watch out for him the way I should have. And I'm sorry."

I chance a look at him, and he is just sitting still, staring at the empty vase on the coffee table. It is painted with faded pink roses.

"I think we need some time with this," Hana says. She clears her throat, but it doesn't help her tremulous voice.

"I wish I could give it to you," I say. "But we're going back to the compound very soon, and you have to come with us."

"All right," Hana says. "If you can wait outside, we will be there in five minutes."

+ + +

The ride back to the compound is slow and dark. I watch the moon disappear and reappear behind the clouds as we bump over the ground. When we reach the outer limits of the city, it begins to snow again, large, light flakes that swirl in front of the headlights. I wonder if Tris is

Shauna sits in the chair again and pushes herself through the doorway. Matthew, Christina, and Zeke follow. I get on last, offering the urn to Shauna to hold, and stand in the doorway, my hand clutching the handle. The train starts again, building speed with each second, and I hear it churning over the tracks and whistling over the rails, and I feel the power of it rising inside me. The air whips across my face and presses my clothes to my body, and I watch the city sprawl out in front of me, the buildings lit by the sun.

It's not the same as it used to be, but I got over that a long time ago. All of us have found new places. Cara and Caleb work in the laboratories at the compound, which are now a small segment of the Department of Agriculture that works to make agriculture more efficient, capable of feeding more people. Matthew works in psychiatric research somewhere in the city—the last time I asked him, he was studying something about memory. Christina works in an office that relocates people from the fringe who want to move into the city. Zeke and Amar are policemen, and George trains the police force—Dauntless jobs, I call them. And I'm assistant to one of our city's representatives in government: Johanna Reyes.

I stretch my arm out to grasp the other handle and lean out of the car as it turns, almost dangling over the street two stories below me. I feel a thrill in my stomach, the fear-thrill the true Dauntless love.

"Hey," Christina says, standing beside me. "How's your mother?"

"Fine," I say. "We'll see, I guess."

"Are you going to zip line?"

I watch the track dip down in front of us, going all the way to street level.

"Yes," I say. "I think Tris would want me to try it at least once."

Saying her name still gives me a little twinge of pain, a pinch that lets me know her memory is still dear to me.

Christina watches the rails ahead of us and leans her shoulder into mine, just for a few seconds. "I think you're right."

My memories of Tris, some of the most powerful memories I have, have dulled with time, as memories do, and they no longer sting as they used to. Sometimes I actually enjoy going over them in my mind, though not often. Sometimes I go over them with Christina, and she listens better than I expected her to, Candor smart-mouth that she is.

Cara guides the train to a stop, and I hop onto the platform. At the top of the stairs Shauna gets out of the chair and works her way down the steps with the braces, one at a time. Matthew and I carry her empty chair after her, which is cumbersome and heavy, but not impossible to manage.

"Any updates from Peter?" I ask Matthew as we reach the bottom of the stairs.

After Peter emerged from the memory serum haze, some of the sharper, harsher aspects of his personality returned, though not all of them. I lost touch with him after that. I don't hate him anymore, but that doesn't mean I have to like him.

"He's in Milwaukee," Matthew says. "I don't know what he's doing, though."

"He's working in an office somewhere," Cara says from the bottom of the stairs. She has the urn cradled in her arms, taken from Shauna's lap on the way off the train. "I think it's good for him."

"I always thought he would go join the GD rebels in the fringe," Zeke says. "Shows you what I know."

"He's different now," Cara says with a shrug.

There are still GD rebels in the fringe who believe that another war is the only way to get the change we want. I fall more on the side that wants to work for change without violence. I've had enough violence to last me a lifetime, and I bear it still, not in scars on my skin but in the memories that rise up in my mind when I least want them to, my father's fist colliding with my jaw, my gun raised to execute Eric, the Abnegation bodies sprawled across the streets of my old home.

We walk the streets to the zip line. The factions are gone, but this part of the city has more Dauntless than any other, recognizable still by their pierced faces and tattooed skin, though no longer by the colors they wear, which are sometimes garish. Some wander the sidewalks with us, but most are at work—everyone in Chicago is required to work if they're able.

Ahead of me I see the Hancock building bending into the sky, its base wider than its top. The black girders chase one another up to the roof, crossing, tightening, and expanding. I haven't been this close in a long time.

We enter the lobby, with its gleaming, polished floors and its walls smeared with bright Dauntless graffiti, left here by the building's residents as a kind of relic. This is a Dauntless place, because they are the ones who embraced it, for its height and, a part of me also suspects, for its loneliness. The Dauntless liked to fill empty spaces with their noise. It's something I liked about them.

Zeke jabs the elevator button with his index finger. We pile in, and Cara presses number 99.

I close my eyes as the elevator surges upward. I can almost see the space opening up beneath my feet, a shaft of darkness, and only a foot of solid ground between me and the sinking, dropping, plummeting. The elevator shudders as it stops, and I cling to the wall to steady myself as the doors open.

Zeke touches my shoulder. "Don't worry, man. We did this all the time, remember?"

I nod. Air rushes through the gap in the ceiling, and above me is the sky, bright blue. I shuffle with the others toward the ladder, too numb with fear to make my feet move any faster.

I find the ladder with my fingertips and focus on one rung at a time. Above me, Shauna maneuvers awkwardly up the ladder, using mostly the strength of her arms.

I asked Tori once, while I was getting the symbols tattooed on my back, if she thought we were the last people left in the world. *Maybe,* was all she said. I don't think she liked to think about it. But up here, on the roof, it is possible to believe that we are the last people left anywhere.

I stare at the buildings along the marsh front, and my chest tightens, squeezes, like it's about to collapse into itself.

Zeke runs across the roof to the zip line and attaches one of the man-sized slings to the steel cable. He locks it so it won't slide down, and looks at the group of us expectantly.

"Christina," he says. "It's all you."

Christina stands near the sling, tapping her chin with a finger.

"What do you think? Face-up or backward?"

"Backward," Matthew says. "I wanted to go face-up so I don't wet my pants, and I don't want you copying me."

"Going face-up will only make that more likely to happen, you know," Christina says. "So go ahead and do it so I can start calling you Wetpants."

Christina gets in the sling feet-first, belly down, so she'll watch the building get smaller as she travels. I shudder.

I can't watch. I close my eyes as Christina travels farther and farther away, and even as Matthew, and then Shauna, do the same thing. I can hear their cries of joy, like birdcalls, on the wind.

"Your turn, Four," says Zeke.

I shake my head.

"Come on," Cara says. "Better to get it over with, right?"

"No," I say. "You go. Please."

She offers me the urn, then takes a deep breath. I hold the urn against my stomach. The metal is warm from where so many people have touched it. Cara climbs into the sling, unsteady, and Zeke straps her in. She crosses her arms over her chest, and he sends her out, over Lake Shore Drive, over the city. I don't hear anything from her, not even a gasp.

Then it's just Zeke and me left, staring at each other.

"I don't think I can do it," I say, and though my voice is steady, my body is shaking.

"Of course you can," he says. "You're *Four*, Dauntless legend! You can face anything."

I cross my arms and inch closer to the edge of the roof. Even though I'm several feet away, I feel my body pitching over the edge, and I shake my head again, and again, and again.

"Hey." Zeke puts his hands on my shoulders. "This isn't about you, remember? It's about her. Doing something she would have liked to do, something she would have been proud of you for doing. Right?"

That's it. I can't avoid this, I can't back out now, not when I still remember her smile as she climbed the Ferris wheel with me, or the hard set of her jaw as she faced fear after fear in the simulations.

"How did she get in?"

"Face-first," Zeke says.

"All right." I hand him the urn. "Put this behind me, okay? And open up the top."

I climb into the sling, my hands shaking so much I can barely grip the sides. Zeke tightens the straps across my back and legs, then wedges the urn behind me, facing out, so the ashes will spread. I stare down Lake Shore Drive, swallowing bile, and start to slide.

Suddenly I want to take it back, but it's too late, I am already diving toward the ground. I'm screaming so loud, I want to cover my own ears. I feel the scream living inside me, filling my chest, throat, and head.

The wind stings my eyes but I force them open, and in my moment of blind panic I understand why she did it this way, face-first—it was because it made her feel like she was flying, like she was a bird.

I can still feel the emptiness beneath me, and it is like the emptiness inside me, like a mouth about to swallow me.

I realize, then, that I have stopped moving. The last bits of ash float on the wind like gray snowflakes, and then disappear.

The ground is only a few feet below me, close enough to jump down. The others have gathered there in a circle, their arms clasped to form a net of bone and muscle to catch me in. I press my face to the sling and laugh.

I toss the empty urn down to them, then twist my arms behind my back to undo the straps holding me in. I drop into my friends' arms like a stone. They catch me, their bones pinching at my back and legs, and lower me to the ground.

There is an awkward silence as I stare at the Hancock building in wonder, and no one knows what to say. Caleb smiles at me, cautious.

Christina blinks tears from her eyes and says, "Oh! Zeke's on his way."

Zeke is hurtling toward us in a black sling. At first it looks like a dot, then a blob, and then a person swathed in black. He crows with joy as he eases to a stop, and I reach across to grab Amar's forearm. On my other side, I grasp a pale arm that belongs to Cara. She smiles at me, and there is some sadness in her smile.

Zeke's shoulder hits our arms, hard, and he smiles wildly as he lets us cradle him like a child.

"That was nice. Want to go again, Four?" he says.

I don't hesitate before answering. "Absolutely not."

+ + +

We walk back to the train in a loose cluster. Shauna walks with her braces, Zeke pushing the empty wheelchair, and exchanges small talk with Amar. Matthew, Cara, and Caleb walk together, talking about something that has them all excited, kindred spirits that they are. Christina sidles up next to me and puts a hand on my shoulder.

"Happy Choosing Day," she says. "I'm going to ask you how you really are. And you're going to give me an honest answer."

We talk like this sometimes, giving each other orders. Somehow she has become one of the best friends I have, despite our frequent bickering.

"I'm all right," I say. "It's hard. It always will be."

"I know," she says.

We walk at the back of the group, past the still-abandoned buildings with their dark windows, over the bridge that spans the river-marsh.

"Yeah, sometimes life really sucks," she says. "But you know what I'm holding on for?"

I raise my eyebrows.

She raises hers, too, mimicking me.

"The moments that don't suck," she says. "The trick is to notice them when they come around."

Then she smiles, and I smile back, and we climb the stairs to the train platform side by side.

+ + +

Since I was young, I have always known this: Life damages us, every one. We can't escape that damage.

But now, I am also learning this: We can be mended. We mend each other.

ACKNOWLEDGMENTS

To me, the acknowledgments page is a place for me to say, as sincerely as possible, that I don't prosper, in life or in books, because of my own strength or skill alone. This series may have only one author, but this author wouldn't have been able to do much of anything without the following people. So with that in mind: Thank you, God, for giving me the people who mend me.

Here they are—

Thank you to: my husband, for not only loving me in an extraordinary way but for some difficult brainstorming sessions, for reading *all* the drafts of this book, and for dealing with Neurotic Author Wife with the utmost patience.

Joanna Volpe, for handling everything LIKE A BOSS, as they say, with honesty and kindness. Katherine Tegen, for excellent notes and for continually showing me the compassionate candy center inside the publishing badass. (I won't tell anyone. Wait, I just did.) Molly O'Neill, for all your time and work and for the eye that spotted *Divergent* from what I'm sure was a giant stack of manuscripts. Casey McIntyre, for some major publicity prowess and for showing me astounding kindness (and dance moves).

Joel Tippie, as well as Amy Ryan and Barb Fitzsimmons,

for making these books so gorgeous Every. Single. Time. The amazing Brenna Franzitta, Josh Weiss, Mark Rifkin, Valerie Shea, Christine Cox, and Joan Giurdanella, for taking such good care of my words. Lauren Flower, Alison Lisnow, Sandee Roston, Diane Naughton, Colleen O'Connell, Aubry Parks-Fried, Margot Wood, Patty Rosati, Molly Thomas, Megan Sugrue, Onalee Smith, and Brett Rachlin, for all your marketing and publicity efforts, which are far too substantial to name. Andrea Pappenheimer, Kerry Moynagh, Kathy Faber, Liz Frew, Heather Doss, Jenny Sheridan, Fran Olson, Deb Murphy, Jessica Abel, Samantha Hagerbaumer, Andrea Rosen, and David Wolfson, sales experts, for your enthusiasm and support. Jean McGinley, Alpha Wong, and Sheala Howley, for getting my words on so many shelves across the globe. For that matter, all my foreign publishers, for believing in these stories. Shayna Ramos and Ruiko Tokunaga, production whizzes; Caitlin Garing, Beth Ives, Karen Dziekonski, and Sean McManus, who make fantastic audiobooks; and Randy Rosema and Pam Moore of finance—for all your hard work and talent. Kate Jackson, Susan Katz, and Brian Murray, for steering this Harper ship so well. I have an enthusiastic and supportive publisher from top to bottom, and that means so much to me.

Pouya Shahbazian, for finding *Divergent* such a good

movie home, and for all your hard work, patience, friendship, and horrifying bug-related pranks. Danielle Barthel, for your organized and patient mind. Everyone else at New Leaf Literary, for being wonderful people who do equally wonderful work. Steve Younger, for always looking out for me in work and in life. Everyone involved in "movie stuff"—particularly Neil Burger, Doug Wick, Lucy Fisher, Gillian Bohrer, and Erik Feig—for handling my work with such care and respect.

Mom, Frank, Ingrid, Karl, Frank Jr., Candice, McCall, Beth, Roger, Tyler, Trevor, Darby, Rachel, Billie, Fred, Granny, the Johnsons (both Romanian and Missourian), the Krausses, the Paquettes, the Fitches, and the Rydzes—for all your love. (I would never choose my faction before you. Ever.)

All the past-present-future members of YA Highway and Write Night, for being such thoughtful, understanding writer buddies. All the more experienced authors who have included me and helped me for the past few years. All the writers who have reached out to me on Twitter or e-mail for camaraderie. Writing can be a lonely job, but not for me, because I have you. I wish I could list you all. Mary Katherine Howell, Alice Kovacik, Carly Maletich, Danielle Bristow, and all my other non-writer friends, for helping me keep my head on straight.

All the Divergent fansites, for crazy-awesome internet (and real-life) enthusiasm.

My readers, for reading and thinking and squealing and tweeting and talking and lending and, above all, for teaching me so many valuable lessons about writing and life.

All of the people listed above have made this series what it is, and knowing you all has changed my life. I am so lucky.

I'll say it one last time: Be brave.

SPECIAL THANKS

In the spring of 2012, fifty blogs helped spread their love for the **DIVERGENT** series by supporting the release of **INSURGENT** in a faction-based online campaign. Every participant was integral to the success of this series! Thank you to:

ABNEGATION: Amanda Bell (faction leader), Katie Bartow, Heidi Bennett, Katie Butler, Asma Faizal, Hafsah Faizal, Ana Grilo, Kathy Habel, Thea James, Julie Jones, and HD Tolson

AMITY: Meg Caristi, Kassiah Faul, and Sherry Atwell (faction leaders), Kristin Aragon, Emily Ellsworth, Cindy Hand, Melissa Helmers, Abigail J., Sarah Pitre, Lisa Reeves, Stephanie Su, and Amanda Welling

CANDOR: Kristi Diehm (faction leader), Jaime Arnold, Harmony Beaufort, Damaris Cardinali, Kris Chen, Sara Gundell, Bailey Hewlett, John Jacobson, Hannah McBride, and Aeicha Matteson

DAUNTLESS: Alison Genet (faction leader), Lena Ainsworth, Stacey Canova and Amber Clark, April Conant, Lindsay Cummings, Jessica Estep, Ashley Gonzales, Anna Heinemann, Tram Hoang, Nancy Sanchez, and Yara Santos

ERUDITE: Pam van Hylckama Vlieg (faction leader), James Booth, Mary Brebner, Andrea Chapman, Amy Green, Jen Hamflett, Brittany Howard, O'Dell Hutchison, Benji Kenworthy, Lyndsey Lore, Jennifer McCoy, Lisa Parkin, and Lisa Roecker

ALLEGIANT

EXTRAS

I set the clippers down on the ledge created by the sliding panel and try to straighten up. He stands behind me, and I avert my eyes as the clippers start to buzz. There's only one guard for the blade, only one length of hair acceptable for an Abnegation male. I wince as his fingers stabilize my head, and hope he doesn't see it, doesn't see how even his slightest touch terrifies me.

"You know what to expect," he says. He covers the top of my ear with one hand as he drags the clippers over the side of my head. Today he's trying to protect my ear from getting nicked by clippers, and yesterday he took a belt to me. The thought feels like poison working through me. It's almost funny. I almost want to laugh.

"You'll stand in your place; when your name is called, you'll go forward to get your knife. Then you'll cut yourself and drop the blood into the right bowl." Our eyes meet in the mirror, and he presses his mouth into a near-smile. He touches my shoulder, and I realize that we are about the same height now, about the same size, though I still feel so much smaller.

Then he adds gently, "The knife will only hurt for a moment. Then your choice will be made, and it will all be over."

I wonder if he even remembers what happened yesterday, or if he's already shoved it into a separate compartment in his mind, keeping his monster half separate from his father half. But I don't have those compartments, and I can see all his identities layered over one another, monster and father and man and council leader and widower.

And suddenly my heart is pounding so hard, my face is so hot, I can barely stand it.

"Don't worry about me handling the pain," I say. "I've had a lot of practice."

For a second his eyes are like daggers in the mirror, and my strong anger is gone, replaced by familiar fear. But all he does is switch off the clippers and set them on the ledge and walk down the stairs, leaving me to sweep up the trimmed hair, to brush it from my shoulders and neck, to put the clippers away in their drawer in the bathroom.

Then I go back into my room and stare at the broken objects on the floor. Carefully, I gather them into a pile and put them in the wastebasket next to my desk, piece by piece.

Wincing, I come to my feet. My legs are shaking.

In that moment, staring at the bare life I've made for myself here, at the destroyed remnants of what little I had, I think, *I have to get out.*

It's a strong thought. I feel its strength ringing inside me like the toll of a bell, so I think it again. *I have to get out.*

I walk toward the bed and slide my hand under the pillow, where my mother's sculpture is still safe, still blue and gleaming with morning light. I put it on my desk, next to the stack of books, and leave my bedroom, closing the door behind me.

Downstairs, I'm too nervous to eat, but I stuff a piece of toast into my mouth anyway so my father won't ask me any questions. I shouldn't worry. Now he's pretending I don't exist, pretending I'm not flinching every time I have to bend down to pick something up.

I have to get out. It's a chant now, a mantra, the only thing I have left to hold on to.

He finishes reading the news the Erudite release every morning, and I finish washing my own dishes, and we walk out of the house together without speaking. We walk down the sidewalk, and he greets our neighbors with a smile, and everything is always in perfect order for Marcus Eaton, except for his son. Except for me; I am not in order, I am in constant disarray.

But today, I'm glad for that.

The *New York Times* bestselling
fantasy series from

VERONICA ROTH

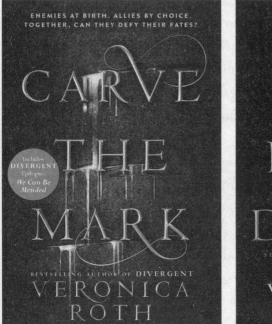

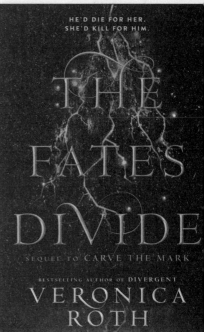

"Roth offers a richly imagined, often brutal world of political
intrigue and adventure, with a slow-burning romance at its core"
—ALA *Booklist*